TEARS TO DANCING

Laura Thomas

Publishers Note:

This is a work of fiction. All names, characters, places, and events are the work of the author's imagination. Any resemblance to real persons, places, or events is coincidental.

Original Cover Art: Evan Scheidegger

DWB PUBLISHING
CHILDRENS LINE

For my daughter, Charlotte-
who will always be my beautiful ballerina...

~ ONE ~

Bethany attempted to open her eyes, suddenly aware of the incredible pain coursing its way through her body. Her head throbbed as she tried to focus on the face in front of her. Aunt Alice's beautiful cheeks were streaked with black mascara. Bethany felt her heart beating wildly when she realized she was lying on a hospital bed, and something was horribly wrong.

"Aunt Alice?" Bethany hardly recognized her own voice. "Where are Mom and Dad? What's going on?"

Darkness engulfed her, swallowing her up into blissful oblivion and the sweetest sleep.

Some time later, she was vaguely aware of soft, rhythmic beeping and felt a desperate need to know what was happening. Frantic, she swiped the long ringlets away from her face and tried to clear her fuzzy head and unscramble memories of the previous evening.

She had been at the Nutcracker Ballet performance with her parents, celebrating her fourteenth birthday. It was a tradition they had shared since Bethany first fell in love with ballet at the tender age of three. Each year since, she dreamed of dancing the lead role as Clara. To make her special day even more magical, a light blanket of white covered the city while they had been inside. Then there was the parking lot, the car. That was all she could remember.

Now Bethany welcomed more sleep and time became irrelevant. As long as she could hide in her dreams, she would believe everything was fine.

"Bethany, honey?" Aunt Alice's soft voice

drew closer and she clasped Bethany's delicate hand, the one without the tubes attached. "It's me, Aunt Alice. Can you hear me?"

Bethany's eyelids felt like lead but she knew she had to rejoin the real world. "What happened? Please tell me." Her voice quivered when she looked up into Alice's emerald eyes, so like her mother's. "Are Mom and Dad okay?"

A female doctor in a crisp, white coat caught Bethany's attention, as she checked the chart at the end of the bed. The doctor met her gaze with concern, and then took several strides around the bed to stand behind Aunt Alice.

Her aunt's voice dropped to a whisper while she cradled Bethany's hand in hers and choked back a sob.

"Bethany, I am so, so sorry. There was an accident. It was really bad. Your leg is broken but you're going to be just fine."

"Where are Mom and Dad?" Bethany asked. "Please tell me."

Alice glanced back at the doctor, then turned to Bethany, and held her close. "There is no easy way to say this, Bethany. They are gone. I'm so sorry."

Bethany felt the blood drain from her face and the room spun around her. She sensed the doctor at her side, checking something.

"Aunt Alice, are you sure? They can't be dead. They're all I have!"

Bethany remembered how anxious she had been last night to get home and open her last birthday present, a surprise her mom had been working on for several weeks. Her precious mom.

Sobs welled up through her body until she

could barely breathe, and she clung to her aunt with all the strength she could muster. Bethany cried for the two most important people in her life—her parents—her best friend and her hero. Suddenly, she wished she wasn't an only child, craving the empathy of a brother or sister, and she longed for the grandparents who had passed away before she was even born. Sensing her world spiraling out of control, she allowed herself to fall back into a long, deep sleep.

Hours later, Bethany still lay in a semiconscious state in San Francisco Hospital PICU, trying to come to terms with her worst nightmare, which was now a reality. Landon and Anita St. Clair were gone forever. She pictured them together just hours ago after the performance. They had carefully made their way across the slick parking lot; Dad, the skinny, tall, blue-eyed blonde with an easy smile, and Mom with her gorgeously thick, chocolate-brown hair and dazzling emerald eyes. Totally opposite, yet perfectly matched.

Feeling a hollow pain unlike anything she had ever experienced, Bethany took time to reminisce on her wonderful childhood that had abruptly ended. Her parents had given her everything she ever wanted in a seemingly perfect world. Then she thought back to the Nutcracker, and how happy she had been walking in the snow, singing carols with her dad, her mom laughing uncontrollably as her father slipped in his new, shiny-bottomed shoes. Now all the family she had was Aunt Alice.

Bethany jumped with a start. "Aunt Alice?"

"I'm right here, honey. Can I get you anything?"

"Where will I go? Who will look after me?"

Bethany crumbled, while yet more tears flowed.

Her mind tried to process her new situation, barely aware of a young, male doctor making his rounds.

"I'll come back a little later," he said gently, and jotted something on her chart.

Alice scooted a chair up close to the bed and tenderly stroked the wayward curls from Bethany's forehead.

"You listen to me. I love you like you were my own daughter. I always have. Everything is going to work out. When you're well enough to be released, you will come home with me. Your mom and dad always planned for that to happen in a situation like this. I would never leave you alone. Right now, you need to stop worrying, and get plenty of rest. Okay?"

"Tell me again what happened last night," Bethany sobbed. "I mean exactly. I don't understand how one minute I was in the car, and now I'm lying in this bed. Please, I really need to know. I need it to make sense."

Alice took a deep breath, and then spoke in slow, measured words, which seemed to choke her.

"You remember starting to drive out of the parking lot? Well, when your dad turned onto the street next to the theater, it was a sheet of ice. I'm sure he was driving really carefully, but it seems he couldn't see beyond a parked minivan.

"Apparently, a big truck spun out of control on the ice, and it came straight for you. Your dad must have hit the brakes, but the roads were just awful, and, well, your car was hit head on. I guess you were a little more protected in the back seat."

Bethany felt her pulse race as she recalled bright lights, screeching metal and a deafening thud. "Why don't I remember the ambulance?"

"You must have been unconscious. That's

probably good, honey. Your mom and dad wouldn't have felt a thing, it happened so quickly. They didn't suffer, Bethany."

Alice blew her nose and wiped at fresh tears. "The doctors took you right into surgery, and I had to sign all the forms when I arrived."

"What happened to the people in the truck?" Bethany braced herself for more bad news.

"There was just a driver, and he's in critical condition at another hospital. I'll try to find out more tomorrow."

Bethany's mind and emotions played tug-of-war at the thought of the truck driver lying injured in a hospital bed. She would never wish anyone dead but why couldn't her parents be injured and alive?

"I just can't believe it."

She winced as she tried to get comfortable on the bed. She knew she must look awful, but for once, she really didn't care at all about her appearance.

"Your leg will heal, honey. I know this will be doubly hard with you not being able to dance for a while."

"For the first time ever, I don't even care about dancing."

As soon as Bethany said the words, she regretted them. Dancing was her life but right now she couldn't even think about that.

She sank back into the soft pillow and realized she had a physical ache right in her heart. Her other injuries, even her broken leg, paled in comparison to the gut-wrenching abandonment she felt. She looked over to her aunt, who was now sitting with her head bowed and her hands clasped gently in her lap. She must be praying.

Bethany loved Aunt Alice fiercely but the young woman was so extreme about her faith. Humble and gracious, she was totally unaware of her own head-turning beauty, and more concerned with living her life "for Jesus."

Alice looked up. "Bethany, I'm going to get myself ready for some sleep. The doctor said I could stay with you tonight. They're less strict with the visiting rules here in the pediatric unit." She picked up a small overnight bag from the floor that Bethany hadn't even noticed before.

"You don't have to, Aunt Alice. I'll be okay."

Bethany felt a gush of emotion and began fitfully sobbing again. It was as if she was no longer able to take charge of her own body, and she had no strength to fight for any self-control.

"I'm not leaving you." Alice cried, clinging to her niece. After their tears subsided, she continued, "The chair pulls out so I can lie down, and quite honestly, I'm so tired I could sleep on the floor. I'm just going into the bathroom for a minute, so you settle down for some serious sleep. I love you, Bethany. And I'm praying for you."

Alice bent down to kiss her niece's forehead but Bethany turned her face before her aunt could see the fresh sheen of tears in her eyes.

Shuddering, she thought about prayer. Religion had been an awkward part of the relationship between Bethany's mom and Aunt Alice, stemming from a conflict many years ago.

Bethany remembered her mom telling her about their parents, Bethany's grandparents, who were missionaries somewhere in Africa. The girls were brought up in a very strong Christian family, and all had gone well until their parents died in a village fire while on the mission field.

The girls were back in the States attending University at the time, and the news shattered them both. Alice found her strength in God, and her faith had blossomed, becoming a huge part of her life. But Anita, Bethany's mother, turned completely away from God, claiming He didn't care about her. She married Landon, another unbeliever, and together they decided they were self-sufficient, and certainly had no desire for God in their lives.

Sometimes Alice talked to Bethany about God and Jesus but her mom never wanted to discuss the subject. Bethany had always believed in God but thought her aunt went a bit over the top. Church was okay at Christmas and Easter but that was enough.

Once the effects of the sedative started to kick in, Bethany struggled to think clearly. This was the last day she would ever spend with her parents, and she didn't want it to end. While she lay in pain, confused, and with a heart full of grief, she decided her mom had been right—God didn't care. And from now on, she wanted absolutely nothing to do with Him.

~ TWO ~

"Bethany, wake up dear. I'm Nurse Mary."

Bethany winced as she attempted to sit up. "Where am I?" she whispered.

"You're in the hospital, dear. They moved you to this private room. Let me help you with that pillow."

The grandmotherly nurse gently eased Bethany's shoulders forward, being careful not to put pressure on her bruised body. Bethany held her breath, remembering the night before.

"Now you may not feel hungry, my dear but you really need to try to eat a little something."

"Thanks." Bethany's throat felt parched and dry from crying. "Do you know where my aunt is?"

Nurse Mary checked the I.V. tubes and swiveled the tray of food over the bed. "Your aunt just popped down the hall for some coffee. The poor girl looks exhausted. I told her I'd stay with you until she gets back. If we get bored, I can tell you some exciting tales of my nursing days back in England. But first, you need something to drink."

She passed a paper cup of water to Bethany and then removed the foil food lids dramatically, revealing a slice of soggy toast, a congealed egg and some orange juice.

"Try and eat up. Unfortunately, hospital food is the same the world over."

Voices floated in from the hallway, and then Alice hurried into the room.

"Bethany," she said. "I'm so sorry I wasn't here when you woke. How are you feeling, honey?"

She kissed Bethany's forehead and settled into the chair next to the bed, clutching a plastic cup of coffee as if it were a life preserver.

Nurse Mary smiled and bustled out of the room.

At the sight of her aunt, Bethany's eyes pooled with tears. "I'm sore all over and my leg aches. I feel like I'm living in a horrid nightmare. I woke up in the night and I'd forgotten about the accident. When I realized I wasn't in my own bed at home, I remembered what happened and that Mom and Dad are gone. Then I felt the cast on my leg and remembered that I can't dance either. Dancing always makes me feel better. What am I going to do? I just want to die."

Alice put her coffee cup on a side table and took both of Bethany's trembling hands in her own. "Honey, this does feel like a nightmare but we'll get through it. I know you never really wanted much to do with God but now might be a good time to reach out to Him."

Bethany slid her hands away, and wiped her eyes and tear-stained cheeks. How could she tell Aunt Alice she didn't want God's help without hurting her feelings? She changed the subject quickly as she suddenly remembered her puppy.

"Oh my goodness, I completely forgot about Muffin! He'll be starving."

"There's no need to worry." Alice squeezed Bethany's hand. "I had a friend collect your little fluff ball yesterday, and he's taking really good care of him. It's too bad I can't smuggle him in to see you though."

"Yeah," Bethany sighed. "I miss him. Which friend gets to be the dog sitter?"

Alice fiddled with her silver, heart-shaped earring and gazed nervously out the window. "Oh, it's Steve, the youth pastor at church. He's a really close friend and wanted to do something to help out."

Bethany eyed her aunt suspiciously and noticed the pinkness in her cheeks. Aunt Alice deserved a good man. Bethany and her mom had tried on numerous occasions to play matchmakers without much success. But how could she possibly be thinking of a relationship at a time like this? Especially with a pastor. Bethany felt an uncharacteristic surge of jealousy, which she tried to push down.

"That's nice of him," she forced out in a murmur.

"Well, now that you know your dog is being fed, how about you eat a little something?" Alice suggested.

"I'm not really that hungry," Bethany replied, and slowly peeled the foil lid from her juice cup. "How can I even think about eating?" She set the cup down as sobs shook her petite body.

Alice held her gently and allowed the torrent of tears to flow once more.

"Knock, knock." A deep voice came from behind the curtain, and a young doctor swished the curtain aside and smiled. Bethany vaguely recognized him from the previous night.

"Bethany," he began, and perched on the end of her bed. "I'm Doctor Thomson. I've been keeping an eye on you through the night. I'm just about to finish my shift but I wanted to see how you are doing."

Bethany reached for a tissue, blew her nose and looked past him.

"Not great," she said finally. "I feel like this is happening to someone else, not me. I've never even been inside a hospital before."

The doctor nodded and softly said, "I can't pretend to know what you're going through, Bethany. It's been a very traumatic night for you but I want you to know we're here to do everything we can to help you and your aunt."

He looked down at the chart in his hand and continued, "You had some pretty nasty breaks in that leg of yours but we were able to repair the damage significantly. I know you probably don't want to hear this but you will have to be patient.

"Breaks like yours take time to heal completely, and we are going to keep an eye on your progress with X-rays and tests. Physiotherapy will be slow at first but hang in there. It says here that you're a dancer?"

"Yes. Dancing is everything to me." She looked into his kind, hazel eyes. "How long before I can dance again, Doctor?"

Doctor Thomson rose from the bed and came closer to her. "I can't make you any promises, Bethany. Everybody heals differently, and your body has been through a lot in the past twenty-four hours. We'll know more in a week or two. In the meantime, you let us know if you need more medication for the pain. Listen to your body, okay?

"I'll check in on you tonight but just call on Nurse Mary if you need anything. She's awesome." He turned to Aunt Alice. "Could I have a quick word?"

"Sure," Alice replied and followed him to the door.

Bethany took a sip of juice with a shaky hand and tried to calm herself down. She closed her eyes and thought of her puppy, imagining him playing in the park on a beautiful summer day. When Alice returned, Bethany put the drink back down.

"What did the doctor say? Not more bad news?"

"No, nothing like that," Alice reassured her. "He just wants me to make sure you take everything very slowly. And there are people here you can talk to if you need a listening ear, like specialists. You know you can always talk to me, and you'll have your friends, too. But sometimes you need an expert to help, you know?"

Bethany thought for a moment, and then asked, "Do you think Natasha knows about the accident yet?"

She pictured her lifelong best friend receiving the shattering news. Natasha had always been the strong one, and had protected Bethany when she was desperately shy through her early years.

"I'm not sure," Alice replied. "I think I should spend some time phoning around today. I'll speak to your school principal, Natasha's parents, your neighbor... maybe she'll take the mail in for a while. I'm pretty sure she has a key."

"Yeah, Mrs. Bennett loves an excuse to be nosey. She's a sweet lady but she has to know everything."

"Oh, Bethany. She's just lonely, that's all. And she really does love Muffin."

"I know." Bethany stifled a yawn and pushed away her revolting breakfast tray. "I'm so tired. You go ahead, Aunt Alice. I'll be okay. These painkillers are making me feel pretty woozy... I think I'm going to take a nap."

Alice smoothed the covers on the bed, threw her purse over her shoulder and headed to the door.

"I'll make those calls and let you sleep. I'm going to pick up Muffin and take him back to my house to settle in. I've got my cell phone, so yell if you need me. The nurses are right outside.

"Nurse Mary is such a sweetheart, I'm sure she'll be popping in to check on you. She may just treat you to one of her stories about London. If you close your eyes and listen to her accent, you almost feel as if you're there. I've already had the pleasure. Anyway, I won't be long. Try to get some rest."

Bethany closed her eyes, hoping her living nightmare wouldn't invade her dreams. Exhaustion overwhelmed her and she was asleep in no time. In fact, sleep consumed the whole day. Alice returned, sat at Bethany's bedside all afternoon, and insisted on staying the night again.

In her waking moments, Bethany neither knew nor cared what time it was. The truth remained the same—she had lost her parents on her birthday, and the fifth of December would be remembered as the worst day imaginable.

~ * ~

"Bethany. Oh, Bethany, can you hear me?" The familiar, shrill voice roused Bethany from her peaceful slumber.

"This is totally disastrous. You poor girl."

"Nat? Is it morning already?" Bethany gasped, feeling disoriented.

Natasha bent over the bed and gave Bethany a long, heartfelt hug. She took the nearby seat and Bethany noticed her friend's immaculate make-up was uncharacteristically smudged. Otherwise she looked like her usual self, wearing a white, faux-fur jacket, designer jeans and white leather boots.

"Your aunt phoned my mom yesterday, and

the doctor said we could come and visit today, so I came as early as possible," she began. "I simply can't believe this has really happened to you, Beth. When Alice told us, we were totally shocked. I've known your mom and dad forever. But you, Beth, what will you do?"

Natasha's pale blue eyes filled with emotion, and Bethany realized that in the ten years they had shared life as "pseudo sisters," she had never seen her best friend so caring.

Bethany rubbed her eyes. "It doesn't seem real, Nat. Can you imagine how different my life is going to be? I've been trying to work it all out in my head, but..."

"You must come and live with us. Totally. Mom and Daddy won't mind a bit. It's not like I have any other sisters or brothers to get all freaked out. I can ask them right now, they're just outside with your aunt."

Bethany burst into tears. Having Natasha come to visit was a healing balm, yet it opened up fresh wounds, too. Every decision was going to be impossible. Even seeing Nat's parents was a painful thought. They had been such dear friends with Bethany's parents for as long as she could remember. She looked at Natasha in desperation.

"Nat, this is all so hard. I'm going to live with Aunt Alice. It's what my parents wanted."

"Oh, Beth, she's so... religious. How much fun will that be? Your mom and dad were great friends with mine. I'm sure they would be happy to have you come live with me."

At that moment, the ugly reality hit Bethany again. "Nat, I can't believe we even have to talk about all this. I just want my parents back."

They spent the next few minutes sobbing quietly together. After a while, Bethany passed the tissue box.

"Oh, just look at my mascara." Natasha cried. "I thought I'd try to cheer you up but now I've made things worse. Bethany, you don't have to make any decisions today. You know how absolutely fabulous I am, and how much fun we would have together. Or... you could go to church with your aunt."

"Did I hear my name?" Alice asked. She entered with a sad smile, followed by the very stylish Mr. and Mrs. Smithson-Blair.

They carried an exquisite glass vase filled with fragrant, yellow roses, and a fluffy white teddy bear. After gentle hugs and condolences for Bethany, Mrs. Smithson-Blair began to cry, and was led out of the room by her equally distraught husband.

Natasha took charge. "Well, Beth, we should go and let you eat some delightful hospital food. Maybe I'll sneak in some of your favorite chocolate brownies next time. We can't have you getting skinnier than me now, can we?"

Bethany rolled her eyes in exaggerated exasperation but literally salivated at the thought of those brownies.

"Bye, Nat. I'll see you soon." She watched Natasha and her parents in a huddle outside the room.

Alice settled down in the armchair next to the bed and reached over to touch Bethany's arm.

"Is everything okay?" she asked.

"Yes." Bethany sniffled. "You know how Natasha is. I love her dearly but everything has to be done her way. She even offered for me to go and live with her."

Bethany peered up through long, dark eyelashes to gauge her aunt's reaction.

"Really? That was kind." Alice's questioning face was both genuine and beautiful. "What do you think about that?"

"Aunt Alice, you are the only family I have left. I want to stay with you." Tears gathered speed as they ran down her face. "Plus, I would never survive Nat twenty-four hours a day, and I'd be living on permanent egg shells in the perfect Smithson-Blair household."

Alice smiled and leaned in close. "Just so you know, there is no danger of any egg shells in the very imperfect Alice Freeman household. You can ask Muffin... he really isn't big on perfection."

And for the first time in two days, Bethany's heart felt a little lighter. Just a little.

"Did someone mention my favorite puppy?" A man's voice came from the open door, and a tall, thirtyish guy sheepishly made an entrance.

"Who are you?" Bethany already guessed he must be the youth pastor her aunt was smitten with.

She was secretly relieved he wasn't some wimpy-looking bookworm, and could understand why Aunt Alice was taken with him. He was a handsome, athletic young man.

"I'm Steve." He approached the bed in two long strides and held out his hand. "Bethany, I just want you to know I am so sorry for what happened. I can't imagine what you're going through. Everyone from church is praying for you."

His piercing blue eyes glistened for a moment, and Bethany shook his hand without saying a word.

"Thanks for coming by, Steve," Alice said, after several moments, breaking the awkward silence. "I think Bethany needs some rest. Why don't we go and grab some coffee?"

Bethany noticed the peachy glow to her aunt's cheeks again and felt that stab of jealousy return.

"Yes, I'll just sleep and leave you two alone." Bethany closed her eyes before anybody could reply.

Late that evening, Bethany stirred from another long slumber. Her aunt sat in the bedside chair reading a thick book, her long, dark hair swept up in a sophisticated knot, revealing her gorgeous cheekbones. Bethany was instantly reminded of her mother, and was hit with a new thought—Aunt Alice lost her only sibling. Bethany had been so absorbed in her own grief, she hardly spared a thought for her aunt.

"Aunt Alice," she said softly. "I'm sorry I was rude to your friend. And I'm sorry you've lost your only sister."

Alice leaned across, and gently hugged her niece, and they wept together.

After several minutes, Alice pulled back and dabbed at her eyes. "I have something to tell you, Bethany. I don't want to bombard you with details but there's something you should know."

Alice took a deep breath and continued, "The truck driver, the one from your accident. I found out his name. It's Tim Bennett... your neighbor's son."

~ THREE ~

Bethany felt a chill flow through her body.

"Poor Mrs. Bennett. Is Tim going to be okay?"

Alice shrugged and tried to smile. "He has some internal injuries that are quite serious but it looks like he's going to pull through. I spoke with Mrs. Bennett earlier today. Bethany, she feels just awful about everything and she sends her love to you. I called the prayer chain at church and they're going to keep an eye on her."

Bethany snuggled down beneath the sheets and allowed herself another good cry. Crying didn't take away the pain but it seemed to be the only way of releasing her new constant companions—anxiety, fear, and frustration.

~ * ~

The next week passed by slowly in a regular rhythm that felt somewhat comforting to Bethany. She spent most of her waking hours talking with her aunt, crying bitterly, watching television, gazing into space, and thinking about her parents. Her favorite teacher from The School for the Arts delivered two novels to catch up on, and assured her she would not fall behind in her studies. This was a slow time academically at a school where the emphasis was on the Christmas dance performances. Even the hospital food was becoming palatable, especially when followed by one of the brownies from a huge basket of goodies, courtesy of Natasha.

Nurse Mary proved to be a real treasure. She was an efficient nurse with many years of experience and looked after Bethany as if she were her own granddaughter. A succession of doctors looked in on Bethany regularly, and a very understanding physiotherapist started her on some basic exercises, as well as working with a set of crutches. All in all, there was a constant flurry of activity in her room, and Bethany felt exhausted most of the time.

Usually, while Bethany slept, Alice was able to use her laptop and continue her work as a magazine writer. She had a very understanding editor who allowed for her special circumstances, and extended her deadlines. The days plodded on, and Bethany's room became smaller as the myriad of flowers, balloons, and teddy bears took up residence.

Several of Bethany's friends from school visited in the evenings and brought her up to speed on what was going on with classes, dancing, and boys. Most people avoided talking about the accident and nobody asked when she would be dancing again. Except Natasha.

"You must be bored out of your brain, lying here for more than a week already. When are you going to come back to school, Beth?" Natasha asked one evening, sitting in the vinyl armchair.

"I don't know. I can't really imagine being in school after everything that's happened. Nothing will ever be normal again, Nat."

"I guess not," Natasha muttered. "But seriously, when are you allowed to dance? Aren't you missing it?"

"Of course I miss the dancing. More than you know. I'm missing a lot of things right now..." Bethany forced herself to calm down.

"Okay, Beth, I get it. I just think it would be a good idea to set some goals for yourself."

"You're right. Maybe after the Christmas holidays, if I'm up to it. As for dancing... I just don't know."

Bethany looked down at the cast covering her entire right leg. Only her toes peeped out, with bright red "festive" toenails, painted by Aunt Alice.

"I hate using the crutches. I'm so clumsy with them. I just hope this wretched leg is mending like it should be. I have a bad feeling about it."

"What do you mean?" Natasha slid her book to the floor, suddenly highly interested in the conversation.

"Well, perhaps it's just because I've had so much happen this past week or so, but I feel like everything is going to keep getting worse. My life will never be the same.

"Sometimes I feel like I'm going to explode because I can't take everything out on the dance floor. You know how I am. That's how I vent, with ballet. What if I'm never able to express myself like that again? I'm not even making sense. I think I'm losing my mind."

"No way, Beth. You've totally lost a lot but you won't lose your mind. You're the smartest girl in school, and everybody wants to be you on the dance floor. Why, you're so smart, you chose me for a best friend! Doesn't get much smarter than that."

Bethany sniffed. "You're right. I'm just feeling sick about the funeral tomorrow. Half of me wants to go, to pay my final respects to Mom and Dad but I think I would break down. I can't use the crutches properly yet, I'm half asleep most of the time, and quite honestly, I don't think I could handle everybody looking at me like I'm an orphan."

"I don't think you should go, Beth. Nobody will blame you. You've been through too much already. I'm going with Mom and Daddy, so I can fill you in on all the details. Actually, Daddy was wondering if you wanted him to video the whole thing. I think it's totally morbid but he said you might want to watch it in a few years or something. I guess you'll be able to see all the nice things people say about your parents. It's up to you. What do you think?"

Bethany furrowed her brow and tried to decide what was appropriate. "Okay, tell your dad he can film it for me. I can let Aunt Alice know. I'm not sure if I'll ever be able to watch it but at least I'll know it's there. And tell him thanks for thinking of me."

While Natasha gushed about the new black outfit she would be wearing, and a nurse checked some charts at the end of the bed, Bethany lost herself in thoughts of her dad. Landon St. Clair would have done the same thing. He thought of everything and everyone. Her heart ached from the inside out as she remembered him. More than anything in the world, she wished she could sit on his lap one more time and tell him she loved him. Now she couldn't even make it to his funeral.

~ * ~

The next day was formidable for Bethany. Alice agreed that Bethany simply wasn't strong enough to attend the funeral and insisted that everyone would understand. Bethany still felt horrible. Truthfully, she didn't want to say good-bye. The funeral was too final, too cut and dried, so she mourned and cried with Aunt Alice. Then she mourned and cried with Nurse Mary while Alice attended the funeral. The only bright moment of her day was when Dr. Thomson told her she could go home the next morning. Her new home, with Aunt Alice.

That night, Bethany wrestled with horrific

dreams of coffins, skidding trucks, and masses of people dressed in black. She was relieved to finally wake up on her last day at the hospital, yet with that relief, came a sense of panic. Since the accident, the daily routine was familiar in this place, and waves of anxiety rippled through her at the thought of an uncertain future.

But this was her life now, uncertain and different. Putting on a brave face, she hurried through her breakfast and daily routine with the nurses.

"I can't believe I'm actually leaving at last," she said. "No offense, Nurse Mary, you've been lovely."

"None taken, my dear. You are one very brave girl, and you have a terrific aunt. Don't you forget that." The plump nurse helped Bethany hobble to her waiting wheelchair. "I'll give Alice your prescriptions when she's finished up the paperwork. Shouldn't be long now."

Nurse Mary hurried into the hallway and Bethany took one last look around her room. It was the place where she wept, grieved, slept many, many long hours, endured the pain of her bruised and broken body, and bonded strongly with Aunt Alice. It was also the place where she had shunned God. She pushed the last thought away quickly when Alice walked in, smiling warmly in spite of the unknown path ahead of them both.

"We're all set to go. As much as I love dear Nurse Mary, I'm not sorry to see the last of this hospital," Alice said in a dramatic whisper.

She came close and knelt in front of Bethany's wheelchair. "I'm so proud of you, honey. I know you're probably scared stiff about the future but let's just take it one day at a time, okay?"

Tears clung to Bethany's eyelashes as she looked down at her angel of an aunt. "That's about all I can manage right now. Every day I get through is a day closer to dancing again." She attempted a faltering smile and clasped Alice's hands in her own. "I just want to see Muffin. Let's go."

Bethany clutched her chocolate brown, fur purse in her hands like a shield, and allowed her aunt to push her through the hallways. She suddenly felt nervous. *This is it. This is the beginning of my new life without parents.*

With her stomach full of butterflies, she smiled at the nurses at the desk, blew a kiss to Nurse Mary and held her breath as they approached the elevator.

"Bethany, are you all right, honey?" Alice asked as they waited for the doors to open.

"I'm fine," Bethany replied with a sigh. "I'm just nervous about going home. I mean, to your house."

Alice slid the wheelchair into the spacious empty elevator and swiveled Bethany around to face her. "My house is your home now, Bethany. It's *our* home."

They began the descent down several floors in silence, along with several anxious-looking visitors on their way out.

When they reached the hospital lobby, Bethany spotted Steve by the entrance. She turned in her chair and with a scowl, whispered, "What's he doing here?"

"Steve offered to help me, Bethany. It took us two trips to bring down the case, flowers, and all your stuff. I'm good, but not *that* good. Please be nice?"

Bethany looked into her aunt's pleading eyes. "I'll try."

Steve wandered over to them, his tousled brown hair sticking up, giving him a cute, boyish look. His wide grin faded slightly when he noticed Bethany's obvious disapproval.

"Good morning, ladies. Your carriage awaits." He bowed deeply, and gained a smile from a blushing Alice.

"Thanks so much, Steve. Bethany and I are more than ready to get going. Is everything in the van?"

"Van?" Bethany virtually spat the word out as if it were venomous.

"Yeah," Steve explained as they made their way through the automatic doors. "Alice wanted me to bring my old van to load all your stuff in. You have a fair amount of luggage to transport here."

"Oh." Bethany realized she sounded very much like Natasha, and she didn't like it one bit. "Well, thanks then. I forgot Aunt Alice's car is so small." Then she quickly added, "But I absolutely love it. Actually, I would like to have a Beetle convertible one day."

Alice laughed. "Thanks but I think you would probably prefer a slightly newer model than mine. Maybe one that is reliable? Not that I'm complaining. We have a lot of awesome memories together."

Bethany took in a deep breath of frigid fresh air and noticed the patches of ice on the parking lot. She remembered the last time she was outside, and the beautiful snowflakes that stuck on her eyelashes when she came out of the theater with her parents. She felt nauseous knowing what followed. Her breath stuck in her throat as she held back a sob.

Alice helped maneuver her into the back seat, and Steve returned the wheelchair. Bethany shivered in her red, wool jacket. She felt a surge of panic creep up her chest when she thought back to the night of the accident. It was the last time she had been in a vehicle. Forcing her fears away, she fixed her thoughts on clipping the seat belt. Her leg was beginning to ache badly and she just wanted to get home. Her new home at least.

Steve drove very carefully, probably sensing the fear of his back-seat passenger. Bethany reminded herself to breathe, especially when they passed any large trucks. Her hands were sweaty, yet she shivered in spite of the heat blowing from the vent. Finally, they reached their destination—a modest but tastefully decorated single story house in a peaceful area on the outskirts of the city. Bethany always enjoyed visiting her aunt here but as they eased onto the driveway, it was a thoroughly weird sensation to know this was her new home.

She saw the place with fresh eyes. The shutters were angled peaks that reminded Bethany of a gingerbread house. The small front yard was immaculate and the oversized red front door almost shouted *welcome*. Bethany knew at dusk, the trees and lines of the entire house would sparkle to life with white lights. Aunt Alice loved Christmas, and her home was always filled with coziness and warmth. It was not exactly the mansion she was used to but Bethany had never been bothered much about material things. Aunt Alice's house was beautiful and warm— just like its owner.

"Let me help you, Bethany," Steve offered, as she hobbled out of the van.

"No, I'm fine. I have to learn to walk by myself with these wretched crutches."

Bethany slowly navigated her way down the short path to the front door, aware of Steve watching her in case she slipped on the ice.

Don't get too comfortable here, bud, she thought. *This is my house now.*

She hated thinking like that but who else was going to watch out for her now that she was an orphan? She needed Aunt Alice more than he did. Too bad if that was selfish. Life was unfair, and she had experienced that in abundance.

"Good job, Bethany." Aunt Alice helped her through the front door and into the living room.

Bethany plopped onto the nearest overstuffed armchair with a footrest and handed the crutches to her aunt. With the flick of a switch, the fireplace was ablaze and Christmas music played softly in the background.

Bethany loved the slightly Mexican feel her aunt evoked in the décor of the house, largely due to the frequent missions trips she had made to Mexico. There were earthy, stone pottery pieces displayed around the room and a collection of black and white photographs in thick, black frames on the wall. Alice artfully snapped beautiful Mexican children with huge grins and dark eyes. Bethany's gaze traveled to the large wedding photo of her mom and dad, and the gorgeous shot of her with her parents from last Christmas. Sadness crept in and she felt a heavy, dull ache inside.

Alice busied herself lighting cinnamon candles and making tea, while Steve carried in Bethany's cases and flowers. Bethany swallowed hard while she watched them trying desperately to make her feel at home.

"Thanks, Steve," Alice said from the kitchen. "Would you mind putting the case in Bethany's room? It's the second door on the right."

Bethany suddenly had thoughts of her old bedroom. She pictured the stunning furniture her dad picked out and bought, and the soft lilac walls her mom lovingly painted for her. *I miss my room, my house, and especially my mom and my dad...*

Like a miniature whirlwind, a black ball of fluff hurled across the living room and barked wildly at Bethany.

"Oh, Muffin, you sweet thing, come up here," Bethany cried. She bent over and reached for the puppy. "I've missed you so much. I hope you've been a good boy for Aunt Alice."

The dog stared into Bethany's eyes and tilted his head to one side in the most adorable way. Bethany laughed, sobbed, and then laughed again as she reacquainted herself with Muffin.

"Is it okay if he sleeps in my room?" she asked, suddenly feeling drained of all energy.

Alice passed the crutches over and said, "I think sleeping sounds like a very good idea. You've had a busy morning. Muffin has already made himself at home on your bed. I knew you wouldn't mind."

Bethany lowered Muffin to the floor, positioned her crutches, and slowly made her way to her new bedroom, with Muffin excitedly running circles around her.

"I have to leave for a church meeting, ladies," Steve shouted from the front door. "I'll check in on you later. Call me if you need anything, okay?"

Bethany rolled her eyes and concentrated on her crutches.

"Thanks, Steve," replied Alice. "And thanks

again for helping out this morning."

"No problem."

Bethany heard the front door slam shut just as she entered her bedroom. She leaned against the doorframe and looked around her new haven. It had been the guestroom but obviously Alice tried to make it a little more special for Bethany. Dark wood floors gleamed beneath a cozy, black area rug and one entire wall of windows was covered with soft, white voile and bordered with rich, brocade drapes. The room was not very large but had a sophisticated French air about it, which was perfect for Bethany.

"We can paint your walls whatever color you like, Bethany, and of course you can have your own stuff brought over, too. Sorry, it's not as big as your old room."

Alice placed Bethany's steaming mug of tea on a coaster on the bedside table and perched at the end of the queen-sized bed.

"At least the bed's big enough."

Bethany moved slowly to the windows and pulled back the voile. Lost in her deepest thoughts, she gazed out at the frosty backyard. Her parents always employed a gardener to keep their shrubs trimmed and lawns manicured but Aunt Alice took pride in doing all the gardening herself. It looked wonderful, too. A perfectly placed porch-swing looked out over paved pathways half-hidden by frost, and shaped bushes and trees that even looked good in winter.

Then Bethany spotted the elegant, stone birdbath standing regally in the corner. She had gone shopping with her mother a few months ago and picked it out for Aunt Alice's birthday. Tears erupted when she realized she would never go on a shopping trip with her mom again.

"I know this is all so hard," Alice whispered. She took Bethany by the shoulders and helped her to the bed. "I can only pray you through this, honey."

Bethany pulled herself away from her aunt's arms in frustration. "I don't want your prayers, Aunt Alice. I want my mom and dad. I want to be able to dance. I want things to go back to normal. Is that so wrong?"

"No, Bethany, it's not wrong. It's just that prayer is the only thing that's holding me together right now, and I only have God to lean on. He's my strength and He can be yours, too."

Alice stood and gently swung Bethany's legs onto the bed and puffed up the white pillow behind her. "Right now, you need to sip your tea and have a nap. We're taking one day at a time, remember?" Alice smiled and left the room.

Bethany wiped her tears with the back of her hand, and took the mug from the table. She looked at the two photos displayed in ornate iron frames next to the coaster. One with her parents looking radiant among palm trees on a beach from their last trip to Hawaii, and another of herself in a white tu-tu, perfectly posed at her last ballet recital.

Bethany felt as if her very soul had been ripped from her, and the pain was unbearable. Muffin jumped onto the bed, and nestled himself in her lap.

"One day at a time," she whispered through bitter tears. "Just one day at a time."

~ FOUR ~

Bethany stretched out on the padded lawn chair and smiled as she listened to her parents playfully waging war in their swimming pool.

"Landon, would you quit splashing me? I can't get any wetter."

Bethany's mom pretended to be upset but quite obviously loved every minute of the water fight with her husband.

"Hey, Bethany, why don't you come and help me? Girls against boys? He won't stand a chance."

"Sure, Mom, I'll be right there."

But when Bethany tried to get up, her left leg felt like cement. The more she tried to heave herself up, the heavier it felt. She started to panic as a consuming weight bore down on her, making it impossible to take a breath. She attempted to call out to her parents but no words came out. Terror and pain enveloped her.

"Bethany. Are you okay?" Aunt Alice stood over the bed and scooped up Muffin.

Bethany caught her breath and blinked back tears for several seconds. "It was just a dream. Sorry if I scared you. Here, I'll take Muffin."

Disappointment shrouded her moment of joy with her parents. It had merely been a figment of her imagination.

"Bad dream?" asked Alice, her face full of sympathy.

"Yeah. No. It was wonderful, actually. Mom and Dad were there. It was only bad when I woke up and remembered everything again."

"Oh Bethany, I'm so sorry. At least you got a good night's sleep. Was the bed comfortable enough for you?"

Bethany sighed and as she stretched her arms up over her head, Muffin jumped down, heading for the open door.

"Really comfortable, thanks. My leg aches but those painkillers seem to help quite a bit. Guess I'm due for another one."

"I'm glad they're lessening the pain, even if they do knock you out for hours at a time," Alice replied. "I've been busy writing an article for work for the past hour and I could do with a break.

"Do you feel like breakfast? I have some pumpkin and chocolate-chip muffins from one of the ladies at church. In fact, I have a freezer full of food from my friends. I don't think I'll ever have to cook again. And trust me, that's a good thing." She helped Bethany up out of bed to go to the bathroom.

"Here's a glorified plastic bag that's supposed to let you take a shower without getting your cast wet. Do you want me to help you with it?"

Bethany grimaced at the thought of putting the bag on her leg but she was desperate for a shower. "Sure. Thanks Aunt Alice. And I'm not that hungry... maybe half a muffin and some tea?"

Alice smiled. "Absolutely. We'll fix you up here and I'll have everything ready for you in the kitchen. Call out if you need me."

Twenty minutes later, Bethany was surprisingly refreshed from her shower and actually feeling quite hungry.

"Everything takes so long with this cast," she complained. "And I'm running out of clothing options fast."

She looked down at her black, designer sweatpants pulled tightly over her cast and collapsed on a kitchen chair. Alice presented her with tea, muffins, and a mandarin orange.

"Bethany, I don't know if you're feeling up to it yet but maybe we should think about going over to your house and picking up some things for you? I'm sure you'd like more of your clothes and maybe some photos, books and..."

"Oh no," Bethany cried, her mouth suddenly dry. "There's no way I can go home. Not yet anyway."

The mere thought of walking through her house without her parents petrified her. It would bring finality to their absence. The family memories screaming out from the walls would be horrific. Right now, Bethany realized she was almost in denial, pretending to have a sleepover at her aunt's house. Her own home would never be the same again. Not with her parents gone forever.

"I just don't think I can do it, Aunt Alice. Please don't make me." Bethany felt like a big baby but she cried anyway. Tears were something she had an unending supply of.

Alice put the dishcloth down and knelt next to Bethany's chair. "I'm not going to make you do anything you're not ready for, honey. I understand, really I do. Steve said we could use his van later today, so why don't you spend some time this morning making a list of what you want, and I'll go over there with him to collect it all. Maybe Natasha will come over to keep you company if we do it after school."

Bethany sniffled and reached for her mug of tea. "I suppose so. I really don't feel like doing much today but I guess Nat could come over for a while."

She looked down and noticed Muffin, on his hind legs, silently begging for a scrap of something delicious.

"Do you think Muffin knows something is wrong?" Bethany put a crumb in her hand, and the puppy devoured it in a split second.

"Dogs are usually pretty smart with picking up on things, honey. He knows you're sad and I'm sure he misses your mom and dad. But I think he's better now that you're home from the hospital. Want me to phone Natasha's mom?"

"Sure. I'll finish eating, and then I'll work on that list. I don't know if you'll find everything I need. Actually, I don't think my room was particularly tidy when I left it. It was my birthday and I didn't bother tidying up..."

Bethany's voice cracked as she realized how thoroughly awful every birthday would be for her from now on. Remembering the day of her birth would always be the date of her parents' death.

Alice put the phone down, sat at the table, and took Bethany's hand. "I know what you're thinking, Bethany. And you're not being fair to yourself trying to imagine what your future birthdays will look like. Maybe we'll celebrate on a different date or something. Every milestone and occasion is going to be tough for you. For me, too. But remember, one day at a time."

Bethany decided to take it a step further and painstakingly got through the day one hour at a time. At four o'clock, Natasha arrived and quickly updated Bethany with all the school gossip, while they curled up listening to Christmas carols by the fire.

"So, how do you feel about your aunt and her new boyfriend being in your old house, Beth? Isn't he like a priest or something?" Natasha admired her fresh coat of scarlet nail polish and passed the bottle to Bethany.

"Nat, he's a youth pastor, not a priest. And I don't particularly like him. I guess I wouldn't like any guy who might hurt my aunt. She has such a tender heart. And I definitely don't like the idea of him being in my house but what else can I do? I just can't go back in that house and see so many reminders of Mom and Dad. Not yet."

Bethany sucked in a breath, and then continued, "I need some of my things, and Aunt Alice knows where everything is kept. He's just the muscle with the van."

"Van? Yuk." Natasha screwed up her face as if she had bitten a lemon.

Bethany recalled her identical reaction to Steve's old vehicle and grimaced. "Try not to be so snobby, Nat. I guess he's just being nice. He is a pastor after all. Probably doesn't have much money."

Natasha's face lit up. "That's it. He's after your money. I bet a bunch of your inheritance goes to Alice, and if he marries her... bingo! He strikes it rich. Oh, that'll be awkward if they get married. I mean, you being here as well. Three's a crowd, you know."

"Hello. We're back." Alice announced from the front door, her arms loaded with boxes. Bethany shot her friend a quick warning look, and then turned to her aunt.

"Hi, Aunt Alice. Did you manage to find most of my things?"

"I think so. Steve's bringing in the rest of it. Thank goodness we had his van."

Natasha rolled her eyes and blew on her nails.

"Hey, Natasha," Alice called out from the

hallway, "would you mind opening Bethany's bed-room door for me, please? I'm a bit weighed down here."

"Oh, but I just did my nails. I guess I can try..." Natasha pouted and then pirouetted down the hallway.

Bethany watched her friend disappear daintily around the corner. She looked down at her ugly cast. *What I wouldn't give to be able to pirouette right now.*

Alice went into the bedroom. "Thanks, Natasha. And thanks for keeping Bethany company while we were out."

She dumped the boxes on the bedroom floor and went back to see if Steve needed any help. He was just coming in with a couple of heavier packages, which he stacked carefully next to the bed, before returning to the living room.

"Wow, girls need a lot of stuff. Hi, Natasha, I'm Steve." He held out his hand but Natasha just gave a wave.

"Sorry, wet nails," she said.

"Oh, okay. How's your leg doing today, Bethany?" he asked, leaning against the sofa.

"It aches and it itches," Bethany replied, and looked at Natasha, who was fussing with her nails and looking very smug.

"So, Steve, what did you think of Bethany's mansion? Ever see anything so fabulous?" Natasha glanced at Bethany, who sent a silent reprimand her way.

"It's very grand. I actually saw it when I collected Muffin while Bethany was in hospital. It's a beautiful neighborhood."

Bethany gave him a stony stare, devoid of

emotion as she processed the thought of Steve entering her house. It was wrong. He should have asked her parents' permission or something. Then she felt silly.

Natasha continued her interrogation. "Well, I hope you had a good look around. It's not like you get to hang out in places like that every day with your job."

Bethany heard Aunt Alice gasp. But Steve smiled and answered, "You're right, Natasha, I don't have a glamorous job. But I wouldn't trade spending time with my youth group for anything. I get to laugh with them, cry with them, do some wild and whacky fun events, as well as sharing the love of Jesus with them. Most are from broken, poorer homes but that doesn't bother me one bit.

"You see, I was brought up in a neighborhood much like Bethany's, and I saw firsthand that money can't buy happiness."

Bethany looked at her friend, who appeared to be speechless for the first time ever. "Oh," was all Natasha could manage.

"I just have one last thing to bring in," Steve added, and winked at Alice, who was busy removing her boots.

"I think I'll make some hot chocolate, it's really chilly out there," Alice said and slipped into the kitchen.

"Was there anything you couldn't find, Aunt Alice?" Bethany called from her armchair, hoping to bring some normality back to the conversation.

"I don't think so. Most of it was in your room, like you said. I can always pop back over to get bits and pieces for you. It's not that far."

Alice came back into the living room and

plunked down on the sofa next to Bethany's chair.

"It was difficult going into the house. It broke my heart. Everything is just how your mom left it. The cleaning service came in and tidied up the kitchen but other than that, it was as if nothing had happened. I think it'll be good for you to go back but only when you're ready. I understand you need time."

"Surprise!"

The tender moment was broken when Steve called from the entrance to the living room holding a seven-foot, perfectly shaped, fresh Christmas tree. Alice joined him and they half-dragged the tree to the perfect spot by the huge bay window.

Natasha sniffed the air and went to take a closer look. "I have to say, it's not nearly as big as ours but it smells totally wonderful. What do you think, Beth?"

Bethany's eyes filled with tears. She thought of the tradition she shared with her parents each Christmas. An immaculately decorated artificial tree would be placed in the living room right at the beginning of December but on Christmas Eve they bundled up and picked out a fresh one from the tree farm nearby.

After it was set up in the family room, they drank hot chocolate while carols blared, and then decorated it together. As the memories heightened, Bethany could feel another sobbing session coming on, and reached for her crutches.

"I'm not feeling so good. I think I'll go lie down. Sorry to leave you all… thanks for coming over, Nat."

Avoiding eye contact with everyone, Bethany maneuvered to her room as quickly as she could. She heard Natasha mumbling something about phoning her parents, and an awkward silence followed.

Bethany shut her bedroom door behind her and sank onto the bed. Tired and in pain, she needed more medication, and she felt guilty about abandoning everyone with the new tree.

Why is everything so painful?

Several minutes later, there was a soft knock on the bedroom door. "Bethany, can I come in for a minute?" Alice's voice was kind and gentle. "I just want to make sure you're okay."

"I'm fine. You can come in if you want."

Bethany didn't attempt to sit up, so Alice sat on the edge of the bed and stroked the ringlets from Bethany's tear-dampened face.

"Natasha's parents are coming to pick her up, and Steve said he'd leave if you want to spend some time decorating the tree with me later. If you feel up to it."

Bethany closed her eyes in despair. "Why does Steve have to be here in the first place? And why does he keep being so nice? What's in it for him? The money?"

Alice's hand froze and Bethany knew her aunt was taken aback.

"Bethany, what are you talking about? Steve isn't after anyone's money. We've been dating for a couple of months now, and he truly cares about me, and you too. He grew up with money, and it became the driving force in his life. Wealth was everything to him.

"When he heard about God's love from a friend, he knew deep down that there had to be more. That's when he put God first, and money was no longer a priority. So you have to know he has no hidden agenda, honey."

Bethany opened her eyes and saw her aunt was crushed. *After all she's doing for me, why am I so selfish?*

"I'm sorry, Aunt Alice. But I really am tired, and I don't feel like decorating the tree. It's too hard. Tell Steve to stay and help you with it. I know you enjoy all this Christmassy stuff. Don't let me ruin everything."

Alice hugged her niece. "You are *not* ruining anything. You are going to be okay. There are so many people praying for you."

Bethany inwardly cringed.

"If you're sure you're all right with Steve helping me, I'll go and get started. Why don't you take a nap and I'll bring some soup in later for you?"

Bethany sat up and Muffin sprang onto the bed next to her. "Aunt Alice, could you just pass me that box on the top of the pile, please? I might unpack a couple of things before I sleep."

Alice carefully placed the box on the bed.

"Just call if you need me," she said from the doorway.

Bethany unfolded the cardboard, and there right on top of the pile, were her prized possessions—beautiful, pink satin ballet shoes. She held her breath as she lifted them up by the ribbons and adored them. This pair had never been worn. Her father bought them for her to hang in her room. But for Bethany, they were her inspiration and represented a very real part of who she was.

Ballet was her passion and her life. The thought of never dancing again terrified her but then she reassured herself that this was merely a broken leg. She would be dancing again soon, maybe even better than before if she worked really hard. She imagined being back at school, complaining about the long, hard, dance lessons and practice times.

I would love to be dancing right now.

Bethany lovingly laid the ballet shoes right next to her sleeping puppy on the bedcover, and delved back into the box. What she saw next took her breath away. She shook slightly when she lifted out a gift wrapped in gold paper and tied in a large, purple bow. Even before she read the tag, she knew this was her special, unopened birthday present. This was the one her mother had been so excited to give her when they returned home from The Nutcracker performance. Only they didn't make it home that night and she would never be able to thank her mother for it.

She cradled the gift in her arms and cried silent tears for this last present she would ever receive from her parents. This was just too much. Too hard. Everything had changed, and it felt like her very life had been sucked from her being. She toyed with morbid thoughts of doing something drastic just so she could be with them again. Shaking her head in despair, she stared longingly at the present, and wondered if she would ever be able to muster up enough courage to actually open it.

~ FIVE ~

After a dreamless night of fitful sleep, Bethany lay motionless in bed and enjoyed a moment of calm. She snuggled her puppy and felt the winter sunshine on her face as it streamed through the bedroom window.

"Just eight days until Christmas... it's going to be awful," she mumbled aloud. "I wish I could just cancel Christmas altogether."

Muffin whined a pitiful moan. "Great, now I've succeeded in depressing my dog. Guess I should get up."

Before Bethany could swing her leg around, Aunt Alice appeared at the open door with a tray in her hands.

"Morning, honey. I thought you might like breakfast in bed today."

"Thanks, Aunt Alice. You don't have to do that, you know. I'm going to start putting on weight if I do absolutely nothing but eat and sit every day. Natasha would love that."

Alice placed the tray on the bed and took over cuddling duty with Muffin.

"Bethany, trust me, you have absolutely nothing to worry about in the weight department. Besides, you'll soon be back in dance classes, practices and recitals, wishing for a restful morning in bed, so make the most of it. Tea, waffles and strawberries... your favorite."

Bethany smiled and then became serious. "Do you really think I'll be dancing again soon? I know some girls have taken months to fully recover from leg injuries." She took a sip of hot tea. "I can't fall behind. It's all I have left."

"I know it's hard but please try not to worry, honey. You have your whole life ahead of you, and right now, you must give your body time to heal. Your heart, too. That'll take longer but I'm here to help you wherever I can. I think my entire church is praying for you, and Steve even has the youth group praying for you, too."

Bethany wrinkled her nose at the thought. "That's weird. People who don't even know me. I'm not sure I'm comfortable with that." She picked at her waffle while she processed the information.

"Well, I can think of the perfect way to help you out with that." Alice smiled. "If you think you're feeling up to a visitor, why don't I ask Sara to pop over for a while later today? I promise you'll absolutely love her."

"Who is she?"

"Sara is the sweetest girl I have ever met, other than you, of course. She's been in Steve's youth group for a few years, and she's exactly your age. But best of all, she adores ballet. She would love to see your photos and things but I also think she'll be a good listener. She's friendly but quiet. What do you think?"

"I'm not sure, Aunt Alice," Bethany said through a mouthful of waffle. "I'm not really good company at the moment. And I don't want anyone praying and preaching at me. I'm just not in the mood."

Alice looked a little dejected. "I understand. Maybe another time. Anything else you'd like to do today?"

Bethany stared out the window at the frosty backyard. She thought about her parents and the crash, and the lucky driver, Tim Bennett, who survived. She thought about the full boxes waiting for her to unpack and her new life in this house. Her heart felt as frosty as the view.

Before she had a chance to change her mind, she said, "Let's invite this Sara over. It might take my mind off things if I have to be nice to somebody. Maybe she'll give me a hand with these boxes, too."

Alice beamed and pecked her niece on the cheek. "You're going to love her, I just know it. She doesn't have to stay long. I'll go and phone her right now."

With that, Alice almost skipped out of the room and disappeared down the hall, her long, wavy hair flowing behind her.

Bethany spent the morning fretting about meeting Sara, surviving Christmas, dealing with her broken leg, and enduring life without her parents. She didn't feel like unpacking her stuff or doing anything with anyone. She was tired of crying, and depression was knocking on the door of her heart with a vengeance.

The doorbell chimed, and Bethany heard Aunt Alice jog to answer it. "Bethany, Sara's here."

Bethany took a deep breath and attempted to shove some unruly ringlets under her headband. Then she grabbed her crutches and made her way slowly and awkwardly to the living room. She rounded the corner and was greeted by Aunt Alice, with her arm around a teenaged girl. At first glance, Sara looked pretty average but then Bethany noticed her exquisite, turquoise eyes.

"Bethany, this is Sara Dean. Sara, this is my wonderful niece, Bethany St. Clair."

"Hi," Sara said in a soft voice. "Thanks for having me over today. I've been looking forward to meeting you. Alice is always showing off photos of her favorite niece."

Bethany was mesmerized by the turquoise eyes but tried to stay with the conversation. "Her *only* niece. Thanks for coming over but I want to warn you in advance, I'm not the best company right now, and I'm likely to burst into tears at any given time."

"Well, don't apologize for that. I can't begin to imagine how you feel." Sara's lovely eyes brimmed with tears. "If you want a good cry, I'll cry with you."

Bethany saw the sincerity in Sara's face, and for a moment she looked just like Aunt Alice.

"Girls." Alice stood with an arm around each of them. "Why don't you get settled by the fire, and I'll make some tea?"

"Actually, Aunt Alice, would it be okay if we hang out in my room? I'd like Sara to meet Muffin, and maybe we could get some of my stuff unpacked later."

Alice looked delighted. "Sure," she said. "I'll bring your drinks in when they're ready. Sara, you are going to love Bethany's puppy."

"I'm sure I will," Sara replied.

Bethany led the way to her room, where Muffin laid on the bed, yawning.

"Oh, he's adorable," cried Sara, curling up beside him.

Bethany positioned herself comfortably on the bed and stroked Muffin's ebony fur. "He knows. And I spoil him rotten but he's my family."

Sara looked at Bethany with genuine sympathy. "You don't have to talk about your parents, the accident or anything if you don't want to. I know it's no comparison but I lost my grandma last year to cancer, and I thought my world had fallen apart.

"If it hadn't been for Pastor Steve, Alice and the others at Youth, I think I would still be hiding in my room. I just know their prayers helped to heal my sadness. Sorry to get all sappy but it might be helpful to you, too."

Bethany twisted a strand of fur in her fingers as she struggled with her new friend's advice. "Well, that's nice for you but I'm really not into God. He hasn't exactly been there for me recently. I don't want to be rude but could we keep Him out of the conversation? I can't handle it right now." Tears pooled in her eyes but she kept them at bay, for the moment at least.

Sara looked up, concern etched on her face. "I'm sorry, Bethany. I don't want to upset you. Just know that if you ever want to chat about anything..." Suddenly, Sara spotted the satin ballet shoes on the dresser. "Oh, those shoes are beautiful, may I take a look?"

Grateful for the change of subject, Bethany nodded. "I've never actually worn them. They're just for show. I have quite a few pairs of very, very worn ballet shoes. Do you dance?"

Sara admired the stunning shoes in her hands and spoke wistfully. "I wish. I took a few classes when I was really little, then they got too expensive for my parents to afford."

The thought of not having enough money for dance lessons was foreign to Bethany, and she was momentarily stunned.

Sara continued, "My grandma saved up and bought me a new pair of ballet shoes every birthday because she knew I loved to dance at home. She even took me to see the Nutcracker a couple of years back. That's my absolute favorite."

Bethany gasped. "No way. The Nutcracker is my favorite ballet, too. I go every year on my birthday with my mom and dad..."

As soon as the words left her mouth, she knew the tears would follow. Strangely, it didn't feel awkward or embarrassing crying in front of a girl she just met. Sara reached over and gave Bethany a comforting hug, embracing Muffin and the ballet shoes.

Bethany realized Sara was crying, too. She grabbed a nearby box of tissues and the pair of them let their emotions run free.

Finally, Sara sniffled her apologies. "Bethany, you must forgive me. I was really hoping to come over and brighten your day a little bit. I didn't mean to bring up something that was so upsetting for you. I'm sorry."

Bethany gazed at the ballet shoes, and then at Sara. There was something remarkable about her. Something other than the color of her eyes. She wasn't dressed particularly fashionably, in fact, she was quite ordinary to look at, except her eyes. She had the same crazy, long curly hair as Bethany, only much lighter, almost the color of honey. But she was natural and genuinely nice.

"Please don't apologize. I'm the blubbering wreck. It actually feels good to cry sometimes, especially when I get to remember my parents. This is all still pretty new for me. Thanks for being my crying partner."

At that moment, Alice came to the door armed with chocolate chip shortbread cookies and mugs of tea.

"Hey, girls, everything all right? I heard some sniffling going on in here." She handed the girls their tea and found a place for the cookies where Muffin wouldn't be tempted.

"Yeah, Aunt Alice. We were just chatting. It appears that everything I think about or talk about involves Mom and Dad, and then it all comes crashing down around me. I don't know if I'll ever be able to have a normal conversation again. But Sara understands me, I think."

Sara nodded and smiled. "Don't be hard on yourself, you're doing so well. What else can we talk about... how about hair? I can't help noticing you have the same riot of ringlets as me. Do they drive you nuts, too?"

Bethany grinned. "Insane. I've tried every product out there but the curls have a mind of their own. I mostly wear it in a bun for school but I'd love to have luscious waves that would hang perfectly down my back like Aunt Alice's."

"Okay." Alice threw her hair dramatically over one shoulder. "Looks like I'm going to get ganged up on by the curly crew. I'll be working in my study if you need me."

Bethany and Sara spent the next hour sipping tea and sharing their life stories. Sara explained that she first met Pastor Steve when she was searching for answers to some big questions. Her childhood was tainted with poverty, sometimes even resorting to begging. Her parents struggled to feed five children, and heartache struck deeper still when Sara's baby brother died from a heart defect.

Bethany had never actually met anyone with such a poor, sad childhood before. But what amazed her more was Sara's joy, in spite of her rotten past.

Bethany though perhaps that feeling had something to do with God.

"Thanks so much for hanging all that stuff up for me," Bethany said, as she sorted the contents of the next box into piles.

"Are you kidding me?" replied Sara. "You have the most gorgeous clothes I have ever seen in my entire life."

Bethany smiled, and realized, not for the first time that afternoon, she lived a very affluent life. There was no hint of jealousy or bitterness from Sara but Bethany was starting to see the temporary nature of having "stuff." What good was it all now that her parents were gone?

She suddenly felt the weight of the world on her shoulders again.

"You look tired." Sara came to the bed and looked at Bethany with a motherly frown. "I really should get going here. Maybe you could take a nap?"

"Oh, I'm fine. Well, maybe a little sleepy. Thanks for helping me with my unpacking. I really enjoyed having you here. It feels like I've known you forever."

"It does, doesn't it?" Sara smiled. "I'm glad your aunt called me. I live really close by, so if you want to hang out again, just let me know." She turned to walk out, and then looked back and whispered, "There's a time for tears but there's a time for dancing, too."

Bethany repeated the words in her mind as Sara left. There was a commotion at the front door, and Bethany closed her tired eyes and listened.

"Who are you?" Bethany recognized Natasha's shrill, demanding tone.

Aunt Alice softly interjected, "Natasha, this is

Sara from my church's youth group. She's been visiting Bethany."

"Hi," Sara said quietly. "I was just leaving. Nice to meet you, Natasha. Bye, Alice. I'll see you at church tomorrow."

"Bye, Sara," Alice called. "And thanks so much for coming. Natasha, you can go on in to see Bethany. She might be a little tired but I'm sure she'll be pleased to see you."

Bethany took a deep breath and pulled herself up to a sitting position when she heard Natasha's footsteps clipping along the hallway. She quickly ran her fingers through her mass of ringlets, suddenly self-conscious about her lack of attention to her appearance today.

"Bethany, who was that girl?" Natasha stormed across the bedroom, carefully placed her huge, white leather bag next to Bethany's ugly cast, and then perched on the end of the bed. "She just doesn't look our type. Did you see those jeans? And I swear she didn't have a scrap of make-up on. Not even lip gloss."

Bethany sighed and looked up at the ceiling. "Nat, would you try to be nice? She doesn't need make-up. Did you not notice those amazing eyes the color of the ocean?"

Natasha pulled a sparkly nail file from her designer purse as if it were a magician's bag of tricks and worked on a flawed nail.

"Yeah, yeah. But she looked so... casual. Where on earth did you meet her?"

Bethany flopped back down on her pillow, her exhaustion kicking in. "Aunt Alice has known her for a few years, and she suggested us getting together today, that's all. She's a really nice girl. She loves ballet and she's easy to talk to. Give her a break, Nat."

"Oh my goodness, your religious aunt is totally trying to brainwash you. It's just as well I decided to drop in on you this afternoon. Did that Sara try to get you to go to church or anything?"

Bethany got defensive. "No, Nat. She was just friendly. Her childhood was rough—she's not rich like us. But she's so happy... I like her."

"Whatever." Silence permeated the room until Natasha's cell phone burst into a frenzied pop tune. She gracefully flicked it open. "Hi. Sure. Sure. Totally. Kisses."

Bethany was developing a headache and her leg began to throb. She made a mental note to take a couple of pills really soon.

"So, Beth, that was Jillian. The girls are heading to the mall. Her dad's arranged this private fashion show thing at one of the new stores. I simply have to go. You look tired anyway.

"I guess your new friend really wore you out. Try a little blush on your cheeks; it'll perk your face right up. Jillian's dad is swinging by for me, so I should go. I'll call you tomorrow and tell you all about it."

And with that, Hurricane Natasha swept through the house and slammed the front door behind her.

"That was a quick visit," Alice said quietly, as she entered the bedroom carrying a glass of water. "Did Natasha have to be somewhere else?"

Bethany yawned. "I actually don't mind one bit. I feel like I could sleep for a week. Nat requires energy, and I'm all out."

Alice smiled and put the water on the bedside

table. "You probably need a little medication and a lot of sleep. I'll order pizza later if you're hungry. Sweet dreams."

Muffin made himself comfortable on the pillow, and Bethany's thoughts wandered to earlier conversations with Sara. She couldn't help comparing Sara with Natasha and was startled to discover she enjoyed hanging out with her new friend much more. Natasha had been her best friend since kindergarten, and Bethany had grown accustomed to the selfish, snobby attitude. But it was getting old, and with everything that happened recently, she wondered if it wasn't time to begin reevaluating what was really important.

Life was certainly short, and there were no guarantees. She couldn't quite figure it all out but there was something about Sara that rang true. There was no hint of falseness, just an honest love for life. It was unrelated to money or academics or looks.

It occurred to her that the cavernous void in her life needed to be filled by something. And she had a horrible suspicion that the *something* had a lot to do with God. She pushed the confusing thoughts away, pulled a blanket over her head, and sobbed angry tears until her erratic breathing slowed down, and sleep finally claimed her.

~ SIX ~

"Rise and shine, sleeping beauty," Alice called. She pulled the heavy brocade drapes aside, allowing grey morning light to fill the room.

"So soon?" Bethany tugged the comforter over her head. "I think I might just stay in bed all day. I can hear the rain, and it's not inspiring me."

Alice swiftly picked up Muffin and deposited him on Bethany's silky pillow. "Your puppy needs some love, honey. You know you can't ignore him. And you did ask me to wake you up bright and early to allow plenty of time to get ready."

Alice curled up on the end of the bed. "You don't have to go to the recital if you're not feeling up to it. Are you having second thoughts?"

Bethany burrowed out from beneath the bedding and sighed deeply. "No. Well, maybe a little. But I figure I have to face everyone sometime, and today is the last day they'll all be together until after the Christmas break. Besides, I want to thank them all for the flowers and gifts they sent. I know they're all worried about me."

Just the thought of going out in the car made Bethany nauseous but she promised herself last night she would go to school today, even if it was just for an hour to catch the show. She wiggled her toes at the end of the cast and tried to push down the bubbling frustration.

It's going to be so hard watching everybody dance except me.

"Aunt Alice, I might just need some time to get my head together. I really think I should go but I'd like to have a few minutes to really prepare myself. Sort of get my emotions in check. Maybe if I spend some time thinking about Mom and Dad now, I won't be such a mess at the recital. Is that okay? Or are we in a hurry?"

Alice leaned over and kissed Bethany on the forehead. "You take all the time you need. There is no pressure for you to be there today, so don't worry if you change your mind. I'll put the kettle on and check in on you later. Love you."

"Thanks," Bethany whispered.

Looking into her aunt's beautiful green eyes reminded Bethany so much of her mom, she almost choked on the pain. Funny how one minute the family resemblance was a comfort, and the next minute it was a cruel reminder of what she lost.

Cleansing, powerful tears came when she imagined her parents at the recital today. How it should have been. Traditionally, her dad always presented her with a special bouquet of pink roses after the show, along with a proud kiss. But not today. Today would be different but Bethany was determined to give it her best shot. She would do it for them.

A little later, Alice hummed and bustled around in the bedroom with breakfast, tea, and an array of clothes in an attempt to keep Bethany's spirits up. After much deliberating and uncertainty, Bethany was ready for her first public outing.

She leaned on her crutches before the full-length cheval mirror and was pleasantly surprised. Her soft, black flared pants covered the cast, and the matching fitted jacket nipped in perfectly at the waist. Her shell-pink silk scarf looked fabulous with the huge, pink leather purse and gloves. Her creamy complexion looked a little paler than usual but she managed to cover the dark rings beneath her eyes.

"I don't know how you tame my crazy curls, Aunt Alice but I must admit I actually love my hair today."

Nobody had been able to make her chocolate-colored ringlets perfect except her mom. The thought brought tears back to her eyes, but she would not have black smudges of mascara ruining their hard work.

"Okay, let's go," Bethany said, with one last glance in the mirror.

"I'll just grab my coat, honey," Alice called from her bedroom. "Wait for me at the front door. It's been raining and I don't want you to slip on the wet path."

Bethany hugged Muffin, slung her purse over her shoulder and put the crutches into action as she headed out. She was scared, nervous, and a little excited. What if she appeared too upbeat? What if she cried her eyes out and everyone felt too awk-ward to even speak to her? This was going to be a tough day.

After some very cautious driving by Alice, the Beetle finally pulled up in the school parking lot. When Bethany gazed up at the school building, her heart felt like it might beat its way out of her chest. Alice trotted around the car in her stiletto boots and helped Bethany with her crutches.

"Oh, my goodness, Bethany, you're shaking from head to toe. What is it?"

"I'm just nervous, that's all. What if nobody speaks to me? It's a bit weird for my friends. They probably don't know what to say. Maybe we should go home."

Alice took one of Bethany's gloved hands and looked deeply into her eyes. "Honey, we don't have to do anything you feel uncomfortable with. It's still early days and I'll willingly take you home if that's what you want. But I know some of your closest friends and they will just want to give you a hug to let you know they care. You don't have to put on a brave face for them. And they will be so surprised to see you here. What do you want to do?"

Bethany looked down at her broken leg and thought about her broken life. "I've got to start somewhere. Daddy always said I wasn't a quitter, and I'm going to do this for him. Let's go inside."

With newfound boldness, Bethany hobbled to the crowded lobby and was instantly swarmed by several teachers and her friends' parents. It was strange to be back inside her school building. Everything smelled foreign, even the familiar odors of stage make-up and rosin chalk. Some of the adults gave her gentle hugs and offered their sincere condolences. Her friends appeared briefly and told her how much they missed her, and were thrilled she came to see the show, then scurried away to do a final warm up before their performances.

As if in a dream, Bethany went through the motions of greeting everyone but on the inside she was shattering piece by piece. By some miracle, she managed to get through the ordeal without breaking down, and then solemnly, she made her way to the small adjoining theater with Alice by her side.

They selected seats at the end of a row where Bethany could be comfortable with her cast, and they could make an early escape if necessary. Alice gave Bethany's hand a reassuring squeeze when the lights went down and the music started playing. Bethany took a moment to close her eyes and clear her head. This was her first official outing without her parents, and it was tough seeing all the families of her friends sitting in the audience.

Why me? Why am I the one who is being punished? What am I supposed to do now with no parents? She realized she was ranting to God and quickly decided to give Him the cold shoulder.

The music started, and Bethany experienced the familiar butterflies in her stomach, like when she waited in the wings before dancing. She memorized most of the dances that would be performed by her ballet class today.

I should be on stage right now, dancing my heart out in front of my parents. This is so wrong.

"You're shaking again, Bethany," Alice whispered, her eyes wide with concern.

Bethany took a deep breath and whispered back, "It's just all so weird. I know this dance inside out, and I want to be on stage."

Losing herself in the music, Bethany watched her friends perform, and endured the bittersweet pleasure and pain of being drawn into the ballet. Even if she wasn't dancing.

But when the final piece of music started, the delicate thread that tentatively held Bethany's emotions together began to unravel. She trembled as she leaned over to her aunt.

"We have to leave now. I'm sorry, I can't do this."

Alice grabbed her own purse and coat. "Sure, honey. I'll bring your purse. You go ahead. Here are your crutches."

As subtly and swiftly as possible, they made their way out of the theater and into the empty foyer.

Thankfully, they were alone at the entrance

when Bethany felt a wave of deep sorrow well up within her and spill down her face. Alice pulled her into a hug and held her tightly while the choking sobs racked her entire body.

When the worst was over, Alice pulled back and spoke softly. "Honey, we are going to get you home right away. Will you be okay for two minutes while I run for the car? It's pouring with rain again. I can bring the car right up to the front doors so you don't get soaked."

Bethany wiped at her eyes, feeling exhausted but grateful that nobody witnessed her breakdown. "I'll be waiting," she said with a nod of her head. "But please, can you hurry?"

Alice waved without another word and dashed for the doors.

Bethany dreaded another onslaught of sympathetic well-wishers. Watching her friends dance had been more traumatic than she could imagine, and the absence of her parents was painfully obvious. While she stood leaning on her crutches at the open doors, Bethany felt a small measure of success. She had made it through a social gathering. Sort of. She looked up at the huge Christmas tree in the corner, filled with sparkling lights and school-made ornaments, and a feeling of dread came over her. Christmas was only seven days away.

One day at a time...

"Beth. What on earth are you doing out here by yourself?"

Natasha's shriek brought Bethany back to reality.

"You're not leaving already are you? We have a scrumptious lunch all set up for everyone. Say you'll stay?"

Bethany looked into the heavily made-up eyes of her best friend and forced a smile. "I can't, Nat. I just can't," she said in a small voice. "I miss it so much."

Natasha hugged Bethany close. "I miss you being here, Beth. We all do." She pulled back and struck a ballerina pose. "But I was totally brilliant, wasn't I?"

Bethany kept the smile plastered on her face, and felt relief wash over her when Alice appeared at the door.

"Bye, Nat. Call me, okay?" Bethany said, as she was whisked away.

"Ciao, Beth. And that scarf is spectacular." Natasha turned to congratulate her fellow ballerinas.

Safely inside the car, Bethany exhaled slowly while the rain washed over the windshield. "Thanks for rescuing me, Aunt Alice." She closed her eyes. The fatigue and emotional stress drained her completely.

Alice turned to her as she waited for the traffic lights to change. "I'm so proud of you, Bethany. Life has changed dramatically for you these past couple of weeks but you are getting through it. I have lots of people praying for you every single day, and I happen to know that God not only hears, and He also answers."

Bethany recoiled inwardly when she thought of her aunt's church all talking to God about her.

He's the one who made the accident happen in the first place.

"Sorry, Aunt Alice but God and I are really not on speaking terms right now. And that's fine by me. He chose to let my parents die, while Tim Bennett got to live. It's so unfair. And Christmas is just one week away. How am I supposed to survive without Mom and Dad?"

Bethany felt heat flood her face and then trickles of tears meandered down her cheeks.

Alice stayed quiet for the rest of the journey home. When they pulled up outside the house, she quietly said, "I love you, Bethany, you know that. Jesus loves you even more. You'll discover that truth one day, I know you will. The last thing I want to do is upset you, so I'll try not to bug you about my faith.

"The problem is it's a huge part of who I am. Each day, I'm relying on His wisdom, and guidance, and strength. I'd be such a mess without Him."

She turned off the ignition and hugged her niece. "How about a cup of tea? I think we both need one."

Bethany sniffed and returned the hug. "Sure, that sounds perfect."

She may have lost an awful lot but Alice was the one ray of sunshine in her miserable life. Even if she did have that crazy, full-on faith. And tea might soothe her soul for a little while but unfortunately, it wouldn't be able to fill the gaping hole in her heart.

~ SEVEN ~

The ordeal of going to watch the school recital left Bethany utterly exhausted. She spent the next day-and-a-half recovering but she didn't regret going. It had been a positive step toward recovery and a good reminder she had a life to return to.

She ached desperately for her mom and dad, especially as Christmas was their favorite time of year as a family. This year, she felt mocked by the season's festivities.

A knock on the door sent Alice scurrying to answer, and Bethany recognized Steve's upbeat greeting. *Great, my life is now complete.*

Bethany shuddered at how bitter she felt toward her aunt's friend. The poor guy hadn't done anything wrong. He always included her in the conversation, tried to help her in every way, and didn't force God down her throat like she imagined he would. He was actually so nice it bugged her.

Plus, it was blatantly obvious he and Aunt Alice were in love. They tried to be subtle but there was no hiding the facts. And that made Bethany uneasy. She couldn't handle any more changes in her life.

"Hi, Bethany." Steve's cheery voice stirred her from her musings. "Ready for a little surprise?"

Bethany laid her book down on the sofa next to a curled up Muffin and immediately thought the worst. *Oh no, they're getting married. What's going to happen to me?*

Alice stood close to Steve, grinning like the Cheshire cat. "Don't look so scared, Bethany, it's a good surprise. At least I hope it is." She turned toward the open front door. "Guys, come on in before

Muffin escapes."

Bethany held her breath as Sara and an extremely good-looking young man walked in carrying paint cans and a ladder.

"What's going on?" Bethany asked, relieved there would be no diamond revealed, and a little overwhelmed by the handsome new guy.

Steve perched on the arm of the sofa and said, "We wanted to paint your bedroom for you since Alice didn't get chance before you moved in. She took a tiny chip from your old bedroom, and I had it matched so you can have a little bit of your old place with you. I have to say, soft lavender isn't a color I would have in my apartment but I think it'll be awesome for you."

His words left Bethany speechless. She realized her mouth was hanging open but she didn't know what to say. She certainly didn't want to start blubbering in front of the painter, young Mr. Dreamy.

"Wow," she finally managed. "This really is a surprise. Thanks, you guys. I loved my old lavender walls. I do kind of miss them."

She struggled to compose herself as she remembered her mother painting her bedroom.

Alice introduced the workers. "You already know Sara, who was more than willing to come and paint rather than go Christmas shopping."

Sara shrugged and blushed. "I just don't like shopping," she said simply. "But I do absolutely love this color of paint. Bethany, your room is going to look beautiful."

Bethany smiled and felt glad her new friend was going to be around today. She could do with some cheering up.

"And this," continued Alice, "is Todd. He's another willing volunteer from youth group who didn't mind getting out of shopping."

Todd went to Bethany and shook her hand politely.

"Hi," he said. "It's really nice to meet you."

Bethany felt her cheeks burn and realized she'd inherited the blushing gene from her aunt.

"You, too," she replied. "And thanks for giving up your time. It's so kind of you. Both of you."

She tore her gaze from his rich brown eyes, the same shade as her own, and looked around at the beaming faces.

"You guys are crazy. It's four days 'til Christmas, and you're here painting my bedroom."

"Think of it as a Christmas gift. Besides, we intend to have fun doing it." Steve flashed a mischievous grin and got up. "First things first, we need to empty most of the room and then cover everything else. This may not look pretty until the very end."

"Let me help," Bethany said, and grabbed her crutches.

"No offense, honey." Aunt Alice took the crutches and laid them back on the floor. "I think we can handle this. It's not easy carrying stuff and walking with crutches at the same time. This is our gift to you, so just relax, read, or watch a movie. You can make occasional encouraging inspections throughout the day. Okay?"

Bethany was about to protest, then remembered Todd in the corner of the room. "Sure," she sighed, picking up her book. "I guess I should try to catch up with this reading for school. Sorry about all the boxes in my room. I haven't quite managed to sort through everything yet."

"No problem," Steve called, as he disappeared with Todd and Alice down the hall. "There's a lot of muscle on this team."

Sara walked through the living room, leaned over the sofa, and whispered, "Bethany, let me know if you need some company. I think Steve's got his project manager head on, and it could be a long, long day." She flashed a smile and quickly joined the others in the bedroom.

Bethany found it hard to concentrate on *The Hobbit* with so many thoughts whirling around in her head. Here she was with her leg in an ugly cast, living in her aunt's house, parentless, confused and hurt. In her new bedroom there were new friends trying to help her come to terms with her new life. She hated new. She longed for the old, the comfortable, and the familiar. Tears pooled in her eyes. These sweet people were trying to give her old, comfortable, and familiar in the form of soft lavender walls.

"I remember reading *The Hobbit* a couple of years ago." Todd's deep, mellow voice caught Bethany by surprise.

She composed herself in record time and turned to him with a sweet smile. "Really? I just can't seem to get into it. To be honest, I'm having trouble concentrating on anything these days."

Todd looked at her with the most sincere eyes she had ever seen. "Bethany, I just wanted to say how truly sorry I am about your parents, the accident and everything. Pastor Steve told us at the youth group prayer meeting just after it happened, and, well, even though none of us actually knew you, we've all been praying for you.

"I was really pumped to be able to do something practical today to help out. I just wanted to let you know."

Bethany swallowed hard and stared at her hands in her lap. "Thanks," was all she could manage.

Several long seconds of silence passed.

"I broke my leg once," Todd continued with a shy smirk. "It's kind of embarrassing..."

Bethany looked up in anticipation of a nice diversion. "Spill. It's only fair. You know my story after all."

"Okay. Well, I'll skip all the gory details. Let's just say I was seven years old, with a thing about being Superman, and there were these stairs that looked like a great take off point."

Bethany burst into laughter as she envisioned the mini superhero in action.

"Hey, Todd." A call came from down the hall. "Is there any danger of a little help with this furniture any time soon?"

"Oh dear," Bethany chuckled. "I'm getting you into trouble with the slave-driver. You better go."

Todd grinned and jogged off to join the workers.

Focus on the positive, Bethany told herself. *I have an aunt who loves me and is happy to have me totally invade her life. I still have my darling little puppy, and my room is being painted by a drop-dead gorgeous guy and a sweet new friend. My leg will heal eventually, and then dancing will become my everything once again.*

She closed her eyes and in her imagination she was on stage at the recital, dancing her heart out next to Natasha, glowing from the inside out as she put her all into every move. With each step perfected, she could almost feel the warmth of the stage lights above her. Ballet really was the most important thing in her young life, so it was no wonder she felt so down. Dealing with the death of her parents would have been slightly more bearable if only she hadn't broken her leg...

"Bethany? Oh, I'm so sorry. I didn't mean to wake you." Sara hovered at Bethany's side with two plates loaded with sandwiches and apple slices. "I thought you were just reading. Shall I put this in the fridge for later?"

Feeling a little disoriented, Bethany pulled herself up. "No, don't worry. I'm actually quite hungry. Is it lunchtime already?"

She accepted the plate and lifted the top slice of bread to discover her favorite, egg salad.

Sara looked at her watch. "It's nearly one o'clock. We're doing pretty well in your room. The first coat is nearly done, so we decided to break for some food. Mind if I join you?"

"Sure," Bethany replied through a mouthful of apple. "Have a seat. You deserve a rest. Where are the others?"

After checking herself for paint, Sara settled onto an armchair. "I managed to finish my first mission, so I volunteered to make lunch for everyone. Steve has it all organized, and it's working surprisingly well. They should be wrapping up soon." She bowed her head to pray silently for a few seconds, and then continued, "I've got some tea brewing. I guessed you might like a cup."

"Thanks, Sara. You're getting to know me well. I wonder where Muffin disappeared. I hope he hasn't been helping with the painting."

"Alice decided it would be a lot safer for everyone if Muffin was napping in her room, so he's happy. Actually, I just peeked in, and he has made himself quite at home on her bed. I don't think she knows yet."

Sara looked up. "How are you really doing, Bethany? Alice told me you went to your school show. That must have been hard for you."

Bethany loved how Sara always made her feel at ease, even talking about the tough stuff. It just felt right opening up to her.

"I'm doing okay, I guess." Bethany lowered her plate. "One minute I think I'm doing a great job dealing with it, and the next minute, I'm a wreck. I try not to dwell on the accident, or the other driver who got to live when my parents didn't.

"People keep telling me time is a healer but I'm beginning to have my doubts. I wish I could dance to get out my frustrations and be me again, then I feel guilty because my mom and dad are gone and I'm whining about a broken leg. Then there's Christmas coming up...."

Bethany could feel the telltale signs of a sobbing session coming, so she stopped and took a deep, cleansing breath.

"I can't even imagine." Sara wiped her fingers on her napkin and in an instant, her look of sorrow ignited into excitement. "I know what you should do. Well, only if you feel up to it, of course. Steve throws an incredible Boxing Day Bonfire Party on the twenty-sixth. It just might help you through the week."

Bethany shook her head. "No offense, Sara but I need a party like a hole in the head right now. I feel so uncomfortable around people, like they don't know what to say to me, and I really don't want to discuss my feelings with just anybody."

Sara came over to the sofa and knelt next to Bethany. "It's such a special evening. It's really casual, nothing too fancy. We'll have a roaring fire with hotdogs, toasted marshmallows, and hot chocolate. But it's so gorgeous. Steve strings thousands of fairy lights on the trees all around us."

Bethany was fascinated but horribly nervous as she imagined this simple, beautiful scene.

Sara continued, "We just chill out really. Steve arranges for a few of the guys and girls to share something special from their lives, or tell the story of how Jesus has changed them." Sara quickly added, "Don't be all freaked out about that. It's just teenagers talking about their lives. Most of the kids have come from horrible homes with rough backgrounds but they have all turned their lives around. Like Todd."

Bethany's eyebrows shot up. "Todd? But he's super-nice. I can't imagine him with any dark, secret past."

"We've all had stuff to deal with, Bethany. Maybe it'll be good to hear how others have dealt with their struggles. I happen to know that Todd is sharing his story at the party. I've known him for years, and let's just say he is truly transformed."

"Wow." Bethany's mind raced with possible scenarios, and she was curious to find out which one was close. "Well, I'll think about it. I guess Aunt Alice will be going."

"She usually comes but maybe she'll stay home with you this year. Unless you change your mind, that is?"

Sara's goofy grin made Bethany smile.

"Okay. I'm going to get that tea poured and then I'll check on the workers." Sara jumped up and disappeared into the kitchen.

Bethany found herself seriously considering the bonfire. A month ago she may have found the idea totally lame but now she was intrigued. First, she would get through Christmas Eve and Christmas Day, and if she had the strength, maybe she would make a quick appearance at the party.

Mom would tell me to go for sure, she thought, as she gazed into the flickering flames of the fireplace. Before her emotions resurfaced, she decided to pay her bedroom a visit.

"Sara, I'm just going to see my room. I'll come back for my tea in the kitchen. And thanks for lunch."

"No problem. Tell them their food is ready," Sara replied.

On the way, Bethany poked her head around the door of her aunt's bedroom, where Muffin stretched out on the big bed in an array of throw pillows.

"He sleeps more than I do," she muttered, and closed the door quietly. A few steps down the hallway, she heard Alice's CD blaring through the shut bedroom door.

"Can I come in?" she shouted.

Someone turned down the volume and opened the door for her.

"Come to check up on us, Bethany?" Steve joked, wiping his paint-smeared hands with a rag. "What do you think? It's just the first coat but it's looking pretty nice so far."

Bethany surveyed the room and smiled broadly. "You guys, it's beautiful. Even with one coat, it's just like my old room. Actually, Aunt Alice, your black furniture will look stunning in here. I might just add a few things from home but I love it. It brings back so many memories. Good memories."

She felt herself tearing up but determined to continue. "You didn't have to do this but I'm so glad you did. Lavender always reminds me of my mom. It was her favorite color. Thanks so much."

Alice, Steve, and Todd gathered around for a group hug, and then Sara slipped in to join them.

"This is lovely," Sara commented. "But isn't anybody hungry? I made lunch, you know."

The group promptly disbanded for a break and Bethany had a moment alone in the room. She breathed in the mix of cool, fresh air from the open windows and the slowly dissipating paint fumes. Tenderly, she lifted the framed photograph of her parents from beneath a dustsheet on her dresser, and held it close

"Mom, you would love this room," she whispered. "And Dad, I'm going to put the special little table you bought me in here. It'll be perfect."

She sighed heavily when her mind wandered to Todd, and she considered his past. What secrets did he have? Would she be shocked? Then, from under the dustsheet she caught sight of the unopened birthday present she had almost forgotten. Still, she couldn't even think about opening it. She couldn't handle any more surprises. At least not today.

~ EIGHT ~

Over the next couple of days, Bethany endured a series of tedious appointments with her doctor, along with more X-rays. She slept in Alice's bedroom to avoid the strong smell of paint in her own, and though her body felt like it was healing, her heart was far from whole.

Christmas Eve morning, she quickly showered, then followed her nose into the kitchen where she found Alice busily making pancakes with fresh strawberries and cream. Pancakes were one of the few culinary delights Alice had truly mastered, and Bethany could tell she was quite proud of them.

"Morning, Bethany. How was your shower?"

Alice's smile lit up the room as usual, and Bethany was again reminded of her mom. Funny how she never really thought about their similarities before the accident. She breathed in the delicious aroma of breakfast. Listening to the carols softly playing, Bethany tried desperately to be positive.

"Lovely. It's getting easier to do stuff. Thanks for sharing your bed with me and Muffin, by the way. I guess we'll be able to move everything back into my room now."

Alice placed a plate of hot pancakes and a mug of steaming tea on the table in front of Bethany. "Sure. Steve is dropping by later this morning to give me a hand with the heavier pieces. But I didn't mind having you guys in my room at all. Muffin seems to have claimed his spot right in the middle of my bed. I bet he's still there."

Bethany chuckled, knowing Muffin was sleeping exactly where her aunt suspected.

Stabbing a succulent strawberry with her fork,

Bethany took a deep breath and made the announcement she had been practicing in the shower.

"Aunt Alice, I would like to visit my old house today."

Alice placed her mug on the coaster and looked at Bethany in astonishment. "Honey, that's great."

Bethany exhaled. "It's Christmas Eve. I hate that it's Christmas Eve and I'm not with Mom and Dad. It was our favorite day. I just want to see our house, look at the tree we decorated, maybe pick up a couple more things. Will you take me?"

"Of course I'll take you, honey. I want to make this Christmas as easy as I can for you."

Bethany suddenly felt selfish. "Oh, what about you, Aunt Alice? I've only been thinking about myself again. Christmas is your favorite time of year, too, and I'm sure you want to go to church, or do something with Steve or your friends. You don't have to babysit me. I've probably wrecked your holiday."

Bethany buried her head in her hands, as Alice leaned over and lovingly held her.

"Do you really think I feel like going out to Christmas parties and being sociable? I've just lost my only sister and my brother-in-law. I want to help you in any way I can, mainly because I love you but also because it stops me feeling sorry for myself. I have lost my entire family, apart from you. You *are* my family, honey, and I'm praying every day for the strength to get through this. It will get easier. It has to."

The two of them cried softly together for several minutes, wiped their eyes, and then attempted to enjoy their Christmas Eve breakfast.

They planned to set out within the hour.

Bethany filled Muffin's dish with dog food, while Alice explained the change of agenda over the phone to Steve. As soon as she set the phone back on its cradle, it began ringing.

"Hello, this is Alice," she said in her usual cheery voice. "Oh, sure, Natasha, I'll pass you over to her."

Bethany took the phone into the living room and mouthed her thanks to Alice. "Hey, Nat, how are you?"

"Other than totally stressing about what to wear to the Christmas Eve party tonight, I'm just fine. Oh, Beth, I wish you were coming. It's going to be fabulous. Mom and Daddy have pulled out all the stops this year, and the caterers are setting up already. Half our class is going to be here, along with all the best looking boys in the city. Are you sure I can't persuade you?"

Bethany rolled her eyes as she explained for the fifth time. "No, Nat, I'm just not up to it. Thank your parents for the invite but I'm going to have a quiet night in and just try to endure Christmas this year."

"Okay. But it won't be the same without you. I have to do the big family thing tomorrow but do you want to get together on Boxing Day? My crazy relatives will still be hanging around but it'll be almost bearable with you here. They like you more than they like me."

Bethany smiled at the truth in her friend's last statement, and then had a flash of inspiration. "Wait, Nat, I have a better idea. Sara, the girl you met here last week, invited me to a Boxing Day party. You should come with me."

"You *have* to be kidding me. First, you refuse

my party, and then you tell me you're going to Sara's? What happened to *I'm just not up to it*?" Natasha's voice reached maximum volume, and Bethany held the phone away from her ear in an attempt to save her hearing.

"Wait, Nat, it's not a "party" party. It's a very casual, low-key thing at the church. And before you start spouting again, it's not actually *in* the church. It's a bonfire party outside. I hadn't decided for sure whether to go but I might feel braver if you come with me. I'd hate to be the only new girl."

Natasha let out an exaggerated sigh. "Well, maybe I'll come. Will there be boys?"

"Natasha."

"Just wondering."

"Actually, yes. And there's this one guy, Todd, who came and painted my bedroom with Steve, and I'm kind of intrigued to get to know him more."

"Oh, I get it. Well, you'll have to fill me in on the details later. I have another call coming in. Ciao."

Bethany sighed as she looked at the phone. "Bye." she said to nobody.

She was surprised at herself for even telling Natasha about the bonfire, let alone inviting her to come. The idea of mixing with strangers from a church made her stomach churn, so she pushed that thought aside and focused on the task at hand. She was going home.

An hour later, Alice parked her Beetle on the circular driveway outside the St. Clairs' house. Bethany wished she had passed on that second pancake for breakfast. She felt nauseous and a little light-headed just looking at the house where she lived her entire life with her parents. It looked strange, different. It was almost as if she had never lived here at all.

Alice took a deep breath and helped Bethany out the passenger door. "Here we are, Bethany. It's a little surreal, isn't it? You okay to go inside?"

Bethany quickly nodded and put her crutches in motion, and she led the way up the path to the grand front door.

Alice shimmied past her. "Here, let me unlock the door for you. Just take as long as you like. We can always come back another day if it's too much."

"I'm okay, Aunt Alice."

Bethany was shocked by the numbness in her own voice, like her body was preparing her for more grief. She shivered when she made her way into the spacious foyer.

"It smells different, don't you think?"

Alice slid her boots off quickly and helped Bethany with her single shoe. "Yeah, I guess it does. I can definitely smell furniture polish. The housekeeper has been in every few days to keep things in good shape. I thought your mom would have wanted that."

Bethany took in her surroundings and felt goose bumps raise on her arms. She looked around at the beautiful, sweeping staircase adorned with festive greenery and the graceful arches of the windows. She hobbled into the great room, and the Christmas tree took her breath away.

Although the multitudes of white lights were not illuminated, the stunning effect of the glistening silver ornaments and the sheer size of the tree were spectacular. She sank into the soft, buttery leather of one of the sofas, and tears spilled down her face.

Alice sat down next to her and took her hand. "After looking at my little tree, this one is pretty amazing isn't it? Your mom loved decorating for Christmas."

"It seems like a lifetime ago when we put up this tree. Me, Mom and Dad. Actually, Natasha was here, too. We were having a sleepover and she joined in with the decorating. Dad got the hot chocolate and popcorn ready while we worked our magic on the tree. It took all evening but we had so much fun. Aunt Alice, what will happen to the tree?" Her voice cracked and sobs took over.

Alice stood, went to the Christmas tree, and reverently slid one of the ornaments from a branch. She came back to the sofa and put the silver globe in Bethany's hand. "Here, honey. You can take a piece of the tree with you."

Bethany held the cool roundness and smiled. "Thanks, Aunt Alice. I'd like that. Mom bought these in Italy. They were her favorites."

"I know, I remember her loving them so much. I'll have all of the ornaments packed up for you eventually. You just take your time. I'll be in the study with the stack of mail. Shout out if you need me, okay?"

"Thanks."

Bethany grabbed her crutches and made her way through the rooms slowly, paying particular attention to the family photographs hung everywhere. She decided to come back for them another time, especially the gorgeous oil painting of her mother in the hallway. She carefully placed the tree ornament into her purse and took a deep breath as she started her ascent up the winding staircase.

"I'm heading upstairs, Aunt Alice," she called

in the direction of the study. Alice's head popped around the doorway immediately.

"Do you want some help?"

Bethany shrugged. "I was going to tackle it myself but now that I've tried one stair, I think it might be a good idea. They're pretty steep."

Alice was at her side in a flash, allowing Bethany to put some weight on her while gripping the iron banister.

"Do you remember when you were little and tried to slide down this banister?"

Bethany grinned. "I wasn't very graceful back then, was I? I must have given Mom so many heart attacks."

"Oh, you did," Alice replied with a chuckle. "But she was just the same when we were kids. She was always the adventurous one."

They reached the landing and Bethany turned to her aunt. "Was she ever as religious as you, Aunt Alice? I mean when she was younger?" Bethany wasn't sure why, but she suddenly needed to know.

"Your mom loved Jesus very much, honey. When we were teens, she was the older, mature one who dragged me to all the youth rallies and Bible studies. Being kids of missionaries, we were always involved with churchy things but your mom always wanted to dig deeper. To know more about God."

Bethany wrinkled her forehead and looked into Alice's sad eyes. "What happened to her?" she whispered.

"Our parents' death hit her really hard, honey. I guess you can identify. It was a tragic accident that devastated us both. They were such wonderful people with a fierce love for Jesus.

"I can't really explain why your mom turned

away from Him but she did. While I drew closer and relied on my faith to get me through, she busied herself with other things and refused to even talk about God. It was so sad. She missed out on so many blessings.

"Didn't she ever talk about it to you?"

Bethany looked down at her cast. "No, not really. She spoke fondly of her childhood, and she loved Grandma, Grandpa, and you but she always looked so sad when the subject of God came up. I guess I'm like her in more ways than I thought." She shuffled off down the hallway in the direction of her old bedroom, and called, "I won't be too long."

Bethany pushed her bedroom door wide open and crossed the hardwood floor to her four-poster bed. She surveyed her belongings, realizing there really wasn't much more she wanted to take. Just the special little ornate table her dad bought for her in France, and maybe a few more framed photos. Unfortunately, she wouldn't need her ballet gear for a while. Looking at the ballet barre that ran the entire width of the room, Bethany caught her reflection in the full-length mirror. She looked small, lost and sad. Her ringlets were having a crazy day and there were dark circles beneath puffy, red eyes.

Wonderful. Nat would have a fit if she could see me now.

Bethany picked up a photo from her dresser. She gazed at herself and Natasha in tutus when they were five years old. She couldn't help smiling at her friend's precocious pose. Nat could be unbearable at times, and utterly self-absorbed but Bethany loved her like a sister. Their mothers had been best friends for many years, and so it was natural for the families to spend lots of time together. Bethany's heart was

heavy as she realized there would be no more vacations with their parents. No more anything with her
parents.

"How's it going, honey?" Alice asked gingerly
from the doorway.

"I loved this room. It was my sanctuary. But
without Mom and Dad here, everything feels so empty and cold. I think I'd like to go back to your place,
if that's okay. I'll come back for my stuff another
time."

"Sure. Let's get you back downstairs."

When they walked past the French doors to
her parent's bedroom, Bethany froze. She stood at
the entrance unable to go inside but wanting just a
hint of her parents. She detected a faint aroma of
Beautiful, the favorite perfume her mother wore
every day. Her dad's sports jacket was folded over
the end of the leather chaise lounge, probably
where he had thrown it in a rush to get ready that
fateful night.

Bethany sagged against her aunt and wept bitterly, as she took in the scene before her. When she
caught her breath, she looked up and whispered,
"Would you mind grabbing Mom's perfume bottle
from the dresser by the window, please? I don't
think I can go in there yet."

"Of course I will. You go on ahead and wait at
the top of the stairs for me, honey."

"Thanks," Bethany replied, and slowly continued along the hallway. Alice caught up, and helped
her down the stairs.

"I'll be so glad to get this cast off." Bethany
sighed, sliding her good foot into her shoe.

The doorbell's chime nearly made her jump
out of her skin. She steadied herself on the crutches

while Alice scurried across the hallway. When she opened the door, a small, frail woman stood before them, her eyes wide with fright.

"Mrs. Bennett," Alice stammered. "How are you? And how's Tim doing? I've been praying for you both."

Bethany felt her stomach knot into a tight ball, her faced flushed with emotion. Confusion overwhelmed her as she battled with compassion, anger, bitterness and regret. Mrs. Bennett had always been a sweet neighbor, baking cookies and taking their mail in when they were on vacation. A busybody for sure but she always meant well. She seemed to have shrunk into herself since Bethany saw her last.

Bethany tried to picture Tim Bennett. She hadn't seen him in ages, probably since she was eleven years old and had a secret crush on him. He had moved out since, and must be in his mid-twenties by now. She shuddered.

Eventually Mrs. Bennett found her small voice. "I'm fine, thank you. And Tim is hoping to come out of the hospital in the New Year if all goes well. Just one more surgery, they say."

She held out her hand to Bethany and continued, "My sweet, sweet girl. Bethany, I don't even know what to say. I am so very sorry. Your parents were wonderful people. Such a horrible accident. Tim is absolutely beside himself. How are you holding up, sweetheart?"

Bethany took a deep breath and put on her brave face—the one she was getting used to now. "I'm okay, Mrs. Bennett." She looked at her aunt for some moral support and continued in a quivering voice, "Aunt Alice is looking after me."

Before she could finish her sentence, her neighbor enveloped Bethany in a surprisingly strong hug, and then the woman took off down the driveway, sobbing and waving profusely.

"Poor lady. She must feel awful," Alice said and   put a comforting arm around Bethany's shoulders. "I'll phone her later, just to check on her. Do you know if she has any other family?"

Bethany shrugged, grabbed her purse, and hobbled to the car. She felt numb, and certainly didn't want to discuss Mrs. Bennett. Of *course she has family. She has her son. I'm the one who has lost everything.*

The drive home was quiet. Once they arrived at Alice's house, Bethany retreated to her bedroom claiming she was in need of a nap. In reality, she just needed a little space to process her emotional morning.

She hadn't considered Tim Bennett much since the accident. She'd chosen to shelve those thoughts until after her time of grief. On the rare occasions when he came to mind, she actually found herself wishing he were dead and her parents alive. She knew it was selfish and evil but facts were facts. She needed her mom and dad so much, and she didn't think Tim was even married. Flashes of dear Mrs. Bennett brought pangs of guilt in waves and Bethany let the emotional roller coaster flow freely in the cascade of hot tears.

This life was too hard. There were too many decisions to be made, and her parents should be here to help her make them. Not for the first time, Bethany fantasized about checking out of life completely. It seemed extreme and dramatic but everything about her existence was extreme and dramatic right now. How she longed to dance again.

Confused and angry, Bethany delved into her purse with trembling hands, searching for a tissue. She pulled several out, and reached back in to retrieve her mom's Christmas ornament. Her kind, beautiful mother would never have such ugly thoughts. Her strong father would never show such weakness of character. She wiped at her eyes, grabbed her crutches while holding tightly to the ornament, and made her way to the living room.

She would hang the stunning decoration on Aunt Alice's cute Christmas tree, she would help get her bedroom back in order when Steve arrived, and she would get through Christmas Eve. Alice promised her a quiet evening later on, with just the two of them by the fire, and some with delicious treats and a seasonal movie. Bethany braced herself and buried her feelings. She could do this because she was kind like her mom, and strong like her dad. Their memory would live on through her.

~ NINE ~

A beautiful, bright Christmas morning broke through Bethany's muddy swirl of dreams. Although she dreaded the thought of facing this particular day, she couldn't help a slight tingle of excitement when she felt a lump at the end of her bed. Aunt Alice remembered her Christmas morning tradition.

Choking back a sob of both gratitude and sorrow, Bethany looked around at her soft lavender walls and patted the empty space on her quilt for Muffin to join her.

"Merry Christmas, Muffin. You get to watch me open my stocking presents, boy. This is the part of the day where it's just you and me."

Bethany's parents began this tradition when Bethany was six years old. She woke up at an unearthly time to open the little presents stuffed into the stocking at the end of her bed. This gave her parents some extra time to sleep in, and Bethany quite enjoyed the solitude before the day of visiting and parties. She could open the gifts all at once in an excited frenzy, or take her time to enjoy each individual unwrapping experience. Today she chose the latter.

Aunt Alice obviously put so much thought into these gifts. Bethany lay each present out carefully on her bed while Muffin jumped back down onto the rug, enthralled with the shiny wrapping paper. With watery eyes, Bethany gazed at the myriad of treasures before her—a pink leather journal, a box of her favorite chocolates, a pair of her mom's silver studded earrings, a framed photograph of her mom and Alice as little girls, a black patent leather wallet, and a gold locket her dad had given to her mom on their tenth wedding anniversary.

Bethany picked up the locket and opened it again. There before her were her parents. Her mom looked stunning in her wedding dress and her dad handsome in his top hat and tails. She sniffed back more tears and went to find her incredible aunt.

Busy in the kitchen, Alice looked lovely, even in her cozy pajamas while humming carols and frying bacon.

"Aunt Alice," Bethany began... but before she could get any words out, her aunt crossed the kitchen and embraced her in a huge, loving hug. Bethany held on tightly, and whispered, "Merry Christmas."

When they finally let go, Alice looked into Bethany's eyes with tears streaming down her own face. "Merry Christmas to you, honey. Did you like your stocking?"

"Oh, the bacon." Bethany pointed over to the frying pan where the bacon was suffering a cremation.

"Not again," Alice cried, rescuing the bacon from the frying pan.

"I can't believe you remembered my stocking tradition. The gifts were totally perfect, Aunt Alice. Thank you so much." She fingered the locket she put on over her nightshirt. "This is so special."

Alice smiled with the kindest, most caring eyes Bethany could imagine, and finished dishing out the bacon with eggs, hash browns and sausages.

"You are so welcome, honey. I have to confess, my gift giving is better than my cooking but this actually looks pretty edible."

They sat down to their breakfast feast, and Alice held Bethany's hand and blessed the food. "Lord, we thank you for this very special day. Thank you for loving us so much that you came to earth for us as a baby, and then died in our place. Please help Bethany in her sorrow. Be her comfort and guide. And thank you for this food and all the blessings you give us. In Jesus' name. Amen."

Bethany heard herself agreeing with an "Amen," and suddenly felt self-conscious. But as she picked at her eggs, she reasoned it was Christmas Day, so maybe she would give God a little credit. Just for today, and just for Aunt Alice.

"So, is Steve coming over later?" Bethany asked.

Alice nodded as she sipped her tea. "Yes, he'll be here this afternoon. Some of the youth from church don't have much of a family life, so he'll hang out with them this morning. Then, after dinner, his family has a big fancy party, so he's expected to attend. He doesn't like the party but he does love his family, so he suffers through it."

"Aren't you going with him?"

Bethany felt guilty at the thought of her beautiful aunt staying home, and not dressing up in a fabulous dress to be out with her boyfriend.

"Bethany, we've been through this," Alice spoke softly, yet firmly. "I really don't want to go to his party, and Steve is absolutely fine with it. To be honest, I like a quieter Christmas Day. It gives me a chance to think about the true meaning of the season.

"And since the Christmas I spent in Mexico several years ago, I can't help thinking of those darling kids at the orphanage on Christmas Day. They were so thrilled with the one present they each received, and the fun little games we played with them. They loved hearing the Christmas story over and over again." She sighed heavily. "I want to stay in with you today, Bethany. Honestly."

Bethany couldn't help feeling a little relieved. She could handle Steve's company for a couple of hours, and she would phone Natasha to wish her family a merry Christmas but other than that, she would lay low today.

She was starting to feel at home in Alice's house, and even though she fully expected more tears throughout the day, it was okay. She could do this.

Several hours later, after watching Alice's favorite Christmas movie, *It's a Wonderful Life*, Bethany stood to stretch and let Muffin out into the yard.

"That was such a tear-jerker, Aunt Alice. I can't believe I've never seen it before. I love old movies."

Alice collected their empty popcorn bowls and headed into the kitchen. "I thought you'd like it. It makes you realize what a difference you make in so many other peoples' lives. It gets to me every single time I watch it."

The doorbell chimed and both Alice and Bethany went to the front door to greet Steve.

"Merry Christmas, ladies." Steve looked sophisticated in his tuxedo, his arms laden with wrapped gifts and a warm smile on his handsome face.

Realizing her mouth was hanging open, Bethany looked at her aunt to see the same reaction. Simultaneously, they burst into laughter and stood back to allow Steve into the house.

"What?" he said, a bewildered look on his face.

Alice composed herself and answered for the

two of them. "Oh, Steve, I'm so sorry. You look... stunning. We're just not used to seeing your James Bond imitation."

Steve dumped his load of presents under the Christmas tree and shook off his jacket. "Trust me, this is not the look I would choose. Mother's Christmas parties require formal dress, especially from me. She even phoned this morning to remind me. Anyway, how about a hug for your own personal James Bond?"

Alice blushed profusely and gave him a tight squeeze.

"I think you look great," Bethany said from the sofa. "We've been to lots of those formal stuffy parties. I feel sorry for the guys. Girls like to get all dressed up, but I think the men would prefer to be in jeans."

"Amen," Steve replied, and sank into an armchair. "You both look fabulous as always... must be something in the genes." He grinned. "So what have you been up to so far today, Bethany?"

His kind, casual manner put Bethany at ease and she gave him a run-down of their Christmas so far.

Alice came in with a tray laden with of mugs of hot chocolate and chocolate-chip shortbread cookies. "I guessed you would be eating later but I thought you might need a little snack."

She passed a mug to Bethany, and Steve took one from the tray. She continued, "We have a small turkey roasting in the oven. We're going to have a late dinner, right Bethany?"

Bethany nodded as she slurped the whipped cream off the top of her drink. "I think we'll have plenty of leftovers, too. I adore turkey sandwiches.

Do you think we could have some for lunch tomorrow, Aunt Alice?"

"For sure. Maybe all week."

Bethany gazed into the crackling fireplace for few moments, and then spoke quietly. "I may even come to your silly bonfire party tomorrow."

Steve put his mug on a coaster and looked up in astonishment. "I didn't know you were thinking of coming, Bethany. That's great. It's an amazing evening. I really think you'll enjoy it."

Bethany smiled coyly as she looked at the eager adults. "Well, it looks like Natasha and I are both coming. But before you get too excited, Nat does have a tendency to change her mind at the last minute, and I'm not totally sure I'd come without her. But it's a definite maybe."

Alice sat on the floor next to Steve's armchair and he put his arm around her shoulder. "Bethany, honey, I think you will love the party. Even if Natasha doesn't come. It's a very special time, and there are already a few kids you'll know. Sara and Todd at least. They'll be thrilled to see you."

Steve nodded in agreement. "It would be even more special with you there."

Bethany looked down at her leg and wished she could get around like normal. She wished she could jump up and start dancing right this minute. Feeling suddenly sleepy, she murmured, "I think I'll have a little nap. It could be a long evening with all the eating and watching Christmas movies."

"Oh wait," cried Steve. "I have something for you."

"Me, too," added Alice, and they both reached under the Christmas tree, retrieving two small wrapped gifts from the pile.

"Oh, you guys didn't have to get me anymore gifts. You've already done so much."

Bethany took the present from Steve and carefully unwrapped it. She opened the lid of the box and gasped. Nestled in red tissue was a beautiful Nutcracker ornament. The little soldier was exquisitely painted, and felt delicate as Bethany held him up.

"Thank you, Steve. It's beautiful. I'll put him on the shelf in my room." Her eyes brimmed with tears. "Did you know the Nutcracker is my favorite ballet?"

Steve smiled. "Yes, Alice told me. I'm glad you like it."

"Here's mine," Alice said and slid an envelope with a huge, green satin bow around it onto Bethany's lap.

Bethany carefully placed the soldier back in its box and slid the bow off the envelope. She looked at her aunt, hoping for a hint of some kind.

"Go ahead, honey, open it up."

Bethany pulled out two tickets and gasped again as her hand flew to her mouth. "Swan Lake. We get to go and see the Swan Lake ballet? With the New York City Ballet Company? They're coming here? Oh, my goodness. Thanks, Aunt Alice."

Bethany reached over to hug her aunt. Alice laughed, obviously relieved at Bethany's response. "We'll go the day after tomorrow. I thought it would give us something to look forward to."

Bethany looked at Steve. "You're not coming, Steve?"

"I think I'll sit this one out. The only ballet I want to see is the one you dance in. How's that?"

Bethany blushed. "Okay. I'll see what I can do

about that. Hopefully you won't have to wait too long." She glanced down at her cast, then continued, "Hey, why don't you both open the gifts I bought... well, Natasha went shopping for me actually."

Steve and Alice were thrilled with their presents—a gorgeous, green silk scarf for Aunt Alice, the exact shade of her eyes, and a pair of soft, brown leather gloves for Steve.

After more hugs, Bethany picked up her gifts and turned to leave. "You guys can have a little alone time. It looks like there are a few more presents under the tree. Have fun at your party, Steve."

Steve groaned exaggeratedly. "Thanks. See you tomorrow."

Bethany closed her bedroom door and collapsed on her bed. Muffin jumped up for some attention.

"Wow," she whispered. "I'm getting through Christmas Day. I really am."

Closing her eyes, she allowed her body to relax, while pondering her day so far. It was certainly different compared to previous Christmas Days but it had been bearable.

She heard the squeals of delight coming from the living room and smiled. Her aunt was one special lady. Maybe it was the crackling fire, the cozy house, or the comforting carols she played that made everything feel better. Or maybe it was something else, like God.

Today Bethany didn't feel angry at Him. It *was* Christmas Day, after all. Steve and Aunt Alice had something very special in their relationships with Jesus—that much was obvious. Today, Bethany would be grateful for her aunt, her friends, her presents, and all the other blessings in her life.

"I wish you were here to share my Christmas, Mom and Dad," she whispered, as she looked down at the Nutcracker ornament, and then clasped the gold locket around her neck. "I miss you. But I think I'm going to be okay."

~ TEN ~

Boxing Day was a flurry of activity at Alice's house—a stark contrast to the mellow comfort of Christmas Day. Alice had been up since the crack of dawn, making trips to the church and helping Steve organize the bonfire party along with some of the kids from youth group. Bethany offered to help but Alice insisted she stay home and take it easy until the party. After reading, watching some T.V., and napping, Bethany decided to invite Natasha to come over early. Hopefully, this would prevent Nat from backing out of the party at the last minute. She took the phone into her bedroom and got comfortable on her bed next to Muffin.

"Hey, Nat, it's me. How was your Christmas?"

"Hi Beth, it was all right I suppose. A bit boring, actually."

Bethany smiled to herself and rolled her eyes. "How come? Too many presents?" she teased.

"Never too many presents, Beth. You know there's no such thing. It was just a long day of visiting with relatives we only see once a year. I wish you'd been here. At least we could've been bored together. But how did it go for you? I mean it must have been so hard."

"I got through it pretty well, I guess. Of course, I spent most of the time thinking about Mom and Dad. How was your big party on Christmas Eve?"

Natasha went into a lengthy, dramatic description of everyone who attended, what they wore, how fabulous or dreadful their hair looked, and how everyone asked about Bethany.

"Beth, everyone misses you. I hope you're not going to stay hidden away for too long."

Bethany seized her opportunity. "That's one of the reasons I called you, Nat. The bonfire is tonight. Remember?"

There was a lengthy pause at the other end of the phone. "That wasn't really what I had in mind, Beth. I guess I could still come. You sure you want to go to a church thing? I mean, how much fun could it possibly be?"

"Nat, you *have* to come. I don't know why but I really feel I should go. I'm not up to a night of fun but I have a feeling this might be just what I need... and I don't want to show up on my own. Please come?" Bethany hated to beg but this was an emergency, and Natasha liked to be wanted.

"Oh, okay. But what on earth do we wear to something like that? It's going to be freezing."

Bethany sighed in relief. "Why don't you come around here in about an hour? Just wear some jeans, boots and one of your gazillion designer sweaters with a warm jacket. You can always borrow something of mine if you want."

"Fine. I'll get Daddy to drop me over. At least I won't have to visit with the neighbors tonight."

"Thanks, Nat. We can drop you home afterwards. See you soon."

"Sure. Bye."

Bethany flopped back onto her pillow, relieved beyond words. She felt braver knowing Natasha would be at her side, and if it ended up being too uncomfortable, she knew Nat's dad would rescue them.

The familiar pang of sorrow cut deep at the thought of Natasha's dad picking them up. Her own dad had always been the chauffeur of the family. He never complained as he ferried Bethany and her friends to sleepovers and movie nights. She missed him so much. Would life ever be normal and painless again?

"Bethany?" Aunt Alice's voice carried through the house.

Bethany picked up her crutches and joined her aunt in the kitchen.

"Hi, honey. I know it's a few hours until the party, so I thought we should eat something now to keep us going. I picked up a pizza—chicken Caesar. Is that okay with you?"

Bethany breathed in the delicious aroma seeping from the large cardboard box. "Oh, yes. I think I could manage a few slices. Nat's coming over in about an hour. Is that all right? I thought it would be a good idea to get her here early."

Alice grabbed a couple of plates from the overhead cupboard and set them down on the kitchen table. "Of course. We'll save some pizza for her. You know your friends are always welcome here. I'm so pleased the two of you are coming tonight." Alice's eyes lit up as she gave Bethany a little hug and poured some cranberry juice into glasses. "Are you nervous?"

Bethany sat down wearily and picked out a large slice of pizza. "To be honest, I'm petrified. I don't normally like going to things I'm not familiar with. But you'll be there, and Steve, Sara, Todd, and Nat. I just hope I don't burst into tears and that Nat behaves herself."

Bethany ate in spite of the churning in her stomach. This evening would be interesting, to say the least.

The afternoon flew by. Bethany helped Alice

sort out napkins, cutlery and plates for the evening, then Natasha arrived and the two of them caught up on the activities of the past couple of days. Bethany reminisced with some tears about Christmases past, while they listened to music and spent an hour getting ready for the party. After changing their outfits numerous times, the girls were finally ready.

"Okay, Aunt Alice, how do we look?" Bethany asked.

Alice looked up from a list she was writing and grinned. "Well, I can honestly say that you two are the most glamorous bonfire partiers I've ever seen." She pushed her long, thick hair away from her face self-consciously. "Actually, I should probably go work on my own appearance. I'll be right back."

Natasha looked Bethany up and down, and then glanced at her own reflection in the full-length mirror. "Hey, Beth, we do look pretty fabulous. I never get the chance to wear this leather jacket, and I absolutely love these fur boots Mom bought me for Christmas. At least my feet will be toasty. I'm a bit worried about your toes peeping out of your cast. Is that little sock going to keep you warm enough?"

Bethany looked down at the sparkly red sock pulled over the end of her foot. "Yeah, I think so. At least it looks festive. You don't think it's too much with the red fur jacket do you?"

Natasha fussed with Bethany's ringlets. "Since when do you question your own fashion sense, Beth? Don't you want to go to this ridiculous party?"

Bethany straightened her shoulders. "I'm fine. And I do want to go. It's just that…. Mom used to always help me with my clothes. I miss her, Nat. It's all so weird."

Natasha delicately hugged her friend, and Alice joined them in the hallway.

"Wow, Alice," Natasha gushed. "It's amazing what a bit of make-up can do, isn't it?"

"Um, thanks, Natasha. I think." Alice shared a secret smile with Bethany.

They all pulled their coats tighter as they headed towards the car in the crisp night air. The church was only a few blocks away, and they were soon pulling into the parking lot.

"If you girls want to go on over to the field, I'll be right behind you. I've got this box to carry. Natasha, could you give Bethany a hand on the uneven grass? Take your time, we're not late."

"Sure thing." replied Natasha. "I hope you know what you've gotten us into, Beth," she whispered.

"Not really," Bethany whispered back. "But it sounds like there are quite a few people already here. Let's try and be inconspicuous."

"Inconspicuous is my middle name," Natasha said with a mischievous glint in her eye.

"Bethany. Natasha. You made it." Steve's voice bellowed across the field as they stepped through an opening in the hedge.

Both girls gasped in unison when they took in the beautiful sight before them. Around a blazing bonfire were huge bales of hay covered in cozy blankets and soft pillows. Every tree in sight was covered in tiny white fairy lights, twinkling like a thousand stars against the black velvet sky. Red patio lanterns hung from branches, casting a warm glow on the Christmassy scene. Carols played in the background and several guys with guitars joined in.

"Hi, Bethany."

Sara's voice brought Bethany back down to

earth and she turned to see her new friend holding two cups of steaming hot chocolate.

"I'm so glad you decided to come. Hi, Natasha, I met you the other day at Alice's house. I'm Sara."

Natasha looked Sara over critically and apparently decided not to answer.

Bethany broke the awkward silence. "Hey, Sara, it's good to see you. This place is fantastic. It's like a little magical grotto."

Sara handed Natasha a drink and held onto Bethany's for her. "I know. I love it. It's the best part of my whole Christmas. It's the same for a lot of the kids here."

"Really?" Natasha squawked in astonishment. "This is the highlight? Oh my."

"Natasha!" Bethany gave her a disgusted look.

Sara shrugged with a smile, and they all made their way to a hay bale.

"My crutches aren't the greatest on grass. Maybe we should sit at this first one."

Bethany couldn't help feeling a little guilty for noticing this spot would be perfect for a quick getaway if required.

"We're just about ready to get started," Sara explained. She handed Bethany's hot chocolate to her. "The guys are going to play a couple of carols and then it's story time."

"Yippee," quipped Natasha sarcastically from behind her drink. "How long does this thing last?"

Sara sat down on the end of the hay bale and replied, "It's up to you, really. We'll all hang out together for the singing and story part. That'll take an hour or so. Most people stay for hot dogs and to watch the fireworks. Some go for sleigh rides."

"Sleigh rides?" Bethany asked curiously. "But there's no snow."

Alice accompanied them on the hay bale and joined in the conversation. "That's where you have to use your imagination. Look over there."

She pointed farther down the field, where two massive Shire horses stood at attention in front of a blanket-laden wagon decorated with white tinsel.

"Wow," Bethany exclaimed. "Steve goes all out for this party, doesn't he?"

Alice glanced over at him proudly. "His parents give him money for Christmas every year, and he spends it on this night for the kids. He even has a gift for everyone when they leave. He really cares about each one of them and wants to give them something special."

Bethany never gave the troubled families in her own city much thought before. She knew her parents gave money to certain charities but being so caught up in her own social life, there was no time to worry about others.

"Hi Bethany." Todd's deep voice caught Bethany off guard.

She looked up and smiled shyly. "Hi, Todd. How are you?"

"Good, thanks. How do you like your new walls?"

She giggled nervously. "I love them." A sharp elbow in her ribs reminded her she was not alone. "Oh, Todd this is my best friend, Natasha."

Natasha flashed him her flirtiest smile, then held her hand out coyly. "Pleased to meet you, Todd. I'm new here."

Todd did his best to hide an amused smirk and

shook her hand. "Hi, Natasha. I'm glad you could both come. You'll have to meet some of the others later. But now, I think it's time to get this thing started. I should get my guitar tuned. See you later."

As he jogged over to the other side of the bonfire, Natasha whispered into Bethany's ear. "You didn't tell me the room painter was such a hunk. This might not be as boring as I thought."

Bethany rolled her eyes and relaxed slightly when everyone began singing *Joy to the World* in glorious harmonies. It sounded amazing, and was followed by *Silent Night*. Bethany looked around and allowed the words to wash over her. Kids raised their faces to the sky and closed their eyes, like they were really singing to God. Even Natasha joined in, enthralled by the beautiful simplicity of the evening.

Finally, Sara sang a solo and her pure, soprano voice filled the air with *O, Holy Night*. Everyone seemed to drink in the meaning of the carol. Bethany had never experienced anything like it.

"Thanks, Sara," Steve said in a voice that carried easily around the fire. "And thanks everyone for coming tonight. We have a few people here this evening who would like to share their stories with you.

"This is not a night for me to preach to you guys, this is a night for you to hear how God changes lives. I'm going to ask Todd to go first." He looked at Todd and grinned. "I've known Todd for a few years, and I know his story will touch many of you. Go ahead, Todd, start at the beginning."

"Thanks, Pastor Steve." Todd looked down at his hands nervously, then stood and faced everyone with newfound confidence. "My story is similar to some of yours. I was born into a home where money was tight and love was absent."

Natasha whispered into Bethany's ear. "Shame. I had high hopes for this one."

"Shh. I want to hear this," Bethany replied. She turned back to watch Todd.

"My dad split when I was a toddler, so Mom had to raise four of us alone. She struggled big time and ended up marrying a guy who beat her. And us."

Bethany gasped. She wasn't used to this sort of thing happening to people she actually knew.

Todd continued, "I don't remember too much, really. Just that he would come home drunk late at night and take out his frustrations on one of us. Mom tried to protect us some nights but he was strong and she was all used up. I think she was just an empty shell, going through the motions of making us basic meals and sending us off to school.

"One night, as I hid in my closet listening to him looking for one of us to beat, I made a decision. I decided I was going to be strong, and that nobody was ever going to push me around again. At the age of eleven, I ran away from home."

This time, Natasha gasped, and then quickly put her hand over her mouth in embarrassment. Bethany gave her an understanding look, and then turned back to Todd, desperate to find out what happened next.

"For the next two years, I lived on the streets. Looking back, I don't know how I survived. Well, I know now that Jesus was watching over me, that He had a plan for my life but at the time it was horrific. I hung out with gangs, begged, stole, slept in alleys and abandoned houses, just doing what I could to survive. It didn't surprise me that nobody came looking for me. It was one less mouth to feed, so I guess my family gave up on me."

Bethany's eyes blurred as she imagined this young boy with no family. She remembered the Superman story he told her, and wondered if anyone cared when he broke his leg. She thought of her own parents who were now absent in her life. But not out of choice. They loved her fiercely, and she still had Aunt Alice to love and protect her.

Poor Todd.

"Anyway, I was doing okay on the streets. I managed to avoid trouble and learned a lot about self-defense and survival. I crashed in all sorts of houses. Friends of friends would take pity on me because I was so young and cute." He flashed a quick, self-conscious smile. "But deep down, I didn't like what I was becoming. I could feel myself harden and knew I was bitter and angry most of the time. That's when I met Pastor Steve."

He looked over at Steve and a huge grin crept across his face. "He was downtown handing out invitations to kids for a big youth rally that was happening at his church. I was just hanging out at the park, looking for trouble when he spotted me. I knew I looked out of place, kind of dirty and full of attitude but he came right up to me and straight away I knew something was going to happen, and that it would be good. I had a feeling."

Bethany struggled to keep her tears at bay but Natasha began to get restless.

"Beth," she whispered. "This is weird. Can we go?"

"Shh, Nat. Just wait 'til he's finished, okay?"

Natasha huffed and folded her arms across her chest.

Todd continued, "Pastor Steve introduced himself and handed me a flier about the rally. I tossed it on the ground, and he picked it up, laughing, and asked if I was hungry. Silly question to ask a thirteen-year-old boy. So the next thing I knew, he was sitting across from me in a burger place, watching me eat like a pig, and asking me stuff about my life. It was as if he cared. He took time out of his day for a complete stranger. For me.

"Nobody had ever done that before, and although I was shy at first about telling him all my garbage, it felt good to share my story with a sympathetic ear. He didn't preach at me or anything but he did invite me to the rally that night. He said he would even come and pick me up from the park. There would be food, so I agreed. As he turned to leave me, he said, 'Todd, you have a Heavenly Father who loves you more than anything. Remember that.'" Todd took a moment to calm his emotions and then concluded his story.

"So I spent that whole afternoon thinking about this Heavenly Father. I decided I wanted to know more about Him and if it was really true that somebody loved me. At the rally that night, my life changed forever. I heard about a God who not only loved me but who died for me and is alive today. No joke, this stuff was just what I needed. I accepted Jesus as my Savior. My life had a purpose. I was loved with an everlasting love, and Pastor Steve and the youth group loved me too, even with all my baggage.

"I got set up in a really cool Christian foster home, where I've lived ever since, and I'm doing pretty well in school, even after missing a huge chunk."

Todd took a deep breath. "I found out that my mom died about a year after I ran away. It's sad. She took an overdose. She never knew she was loved. My stepdad disappeared but I am in touch with my siblings, and they're all in foster care, too.

"I've been able to forgive, and now I live my life knowing that my Heavenly Father really does love me more than anything. Me standing here tonight is living proof of that." He smiled as he looked around at the faces glowing in the fire's reflection. "You guys all have a Heavenly Father who loves you more than anything, too."

Suddenly, Bethany grabbed Natasha's arm and whispered, "Phone your dad, now. Please, I can't stay here." Tears streamed down her face in torrents. "Please, take me home."

~ ELEVEN ~

Natasha swiftly scooped up their purses.
Bethany hopped off the hay bale, and they hurried
across the field, far away from the excited crowd of
teenagers.

"Wait, Bethany," Alice shouted, catching up
with them. "What's wrong?"

Natasha stood at Bethany's side and answered
for her. "We're going home. Daddy is on his way.
This church stuff simply isn't for us, and now Beth's
all upset. I don't know what you were thinking,
tricking us into believing this would be fun."

Alice looked as if she'd been slapped in the
face.

Bethany scowled at Natasha, took a deep
breath, and spoke in sobs. "Aunt Alice, that's not
true. Nat, you can't speak to my aunt like that, you
just can't. The fact is, I was really enjoying the
whole thing but I need to go and think about Todd's
story. You may not believe him, Nat, but I do. As
much as I'm angry with God right now, the idea of a
Heavenly Father gives me butterflies in the pit of my
stomach. I just need to go home and think."

Bethany gazed at the two faces before her.
Natasha's squinted eyes seemed to be accusing her
of betrayal, whereas Aunt Alice's were full of love
and compassion.

"Well, are you coming or not?" Natasha de-
manded, her hands on her hips.

Bethany bit her lip nervously and then turned
to her aunt. "If it's okay, Aunt Alice, could you give
me a ride home, please?"

Alice put her arm around Bethany and replied
softly, "Of course, honey." She turned to Natasha

and continued, "I'm really sorry you didn't enjoy the evening, Natasha. I certainly didn't mean to upset you. Would you like me to drop you home, too?"

Natasha handed Bethany her purse and shrugged hers over her shoulder before answering in a monotone voice. "No. Daddy's on his way. Goodnight."

Bethany reached out and touched Natasha's arm. "Nat," she whispered, "Don't be mad at me. I have so much stuff in my head. It feels like I'm going to explode. I'll call you tomorrow, okay?"

Natasha nodded, and all three of them walked silently to the street, leaving behind the sounds of teenagers sharing their hearts around a crackling fire.

~ * ~

The short ride home was wordless, and as Alice helped Bethany through the front door, Bethany welcomed the feeling of relief that came from simply being home.

"Aunt Alice," she began. "I really think this is starting to feel like home." New tears brimmed as she breathed in the scent of cinnamon and Christmas. "Thank you for being so patient with me. Todd had no one but even though my mom and dad are gone…"

She fell into her aunt's embrace and cried with all her might, unable to complete her thought.

Alice rubbed Bethany's back softly and cried along with her. "You know you have many people who care, don't you?" she said in a soft, soothing voice. "You still have all your friends, some new ones, too. Steve adores you, and tonight was a good reminder that someone else loves you, too. Someone who will never, ever leave you."

Bethany stood back, searching her aunt's face. "I know," she whispered. "I know. I don't understand but after listening to Todd tonight, I have a lot to process. Goodnight, Aunt Alice."

Alice gave her one last hug and said, "Sweet dreams, honey. You know I'm always here if you want to talk."

Bethany quickly readied herself for bed. She lay her head down on the soft pillow and tried to slow the myriad of thoughts and images swirling through her mind.

Flashes of her mom and dad smiling at her from their swimming pool in the backyard were followed by Todd as a little Superman with nobody to catch him. Suddenly, Aunt Alice and Steve were getting married, and then Natasha was dancing furiously on a stage. Each separate scenario mingled randomly with the others, and Bethany felt breathless, finding herself running from one to the other, wanting to be there for everyone. She felt helpless and hopeless, until an all-consuming warmth wrapped around her like a blanket, and she was finally able to rest.

~ * ~

Bethany stretched and opened one eye, glancing at her alarm clock. She groaned in disbelief. "Muffin, why didn't you wake me, boy?" she said to the mound of fur lying beside her. "It's lunch time. Apparently, I needed a lot of sleep."

Bethany felt considerably fresher after a long shower. She dressed in comfortable chocolate brown yoga pants and matching top, then limped to the kitchen, where she found Steve making grilled cheese sandwiches.

"Hi, Steve," she said sheepishly. "I guess I missed breakfast." She poured herself a glass of cranberry juice and sat at the table.

Steve turned and grinned. "That might not be a bad thing," he replied. "I got here just in time to rescue the sandwiches from your aunt's culinary kiss of death."

"Hey!"

Bethany and Steve both turned to see Aunt Alice at the doorway, looking most indignant with a huge, fake pout.

"I'm improving slowly with my cooking skills, okay? These things take time and practice." She flicked Steve with the edge of a dishcloth as she walked past him and he retaliated by planting a quick kiss of apology on her cheek.

"Forgiven," Alice muttered, blushing profusely.

Steve placed a plate in front of Bethany and her mouth watered. The grilled cheese sandwiches were daintily cut and arranged alongside slices of fresh cantaloupe, black grapes, and strawberries.

"Where did you learn to put a meal together so well, Steve?" Bethany asked and popped a grape into her mouth.

"We had a housekeeper when I was growing up," he answered, and continued to grill more sandwiches. "I loved to be down in the kitchen, watching the amazing dishes she created. Sometimes she'd let me help."

Alice sat down next to Bethany with a cup of coffee. "So, Bethany, I guess you got a pretty good night's sleep after all? I didn't want to disturb you this morning, seeing how we'll have a late night tonight."

"We will?" Bethany questioned. "How come?"

"Bethany St. Clair, did you forget about Swan

Lake?"

Bethany almost choked on a grape. "I totally did. Oh my goodness, what time will we leave?"

"Around five o'clock. I thought we could have a nice Italian dinner at *Ricardo's* on the way, if you feel up to it," Aunt Alice answered.

"So not fair," Steve groaned in mock protest. "That's my favorite restaurant."

Bethany grinned. "You could always join us for dinner. Even if you are too chicken to go the ballet with us."

Steve set the rest of the lunch on the table and said, "Thanks for the invite, Bethany, I really am honored. I thought this was just for the two of you but of course I'll come if you think you'll need me there...."

Bethany bit her lower lip and looked at her aunt. "I think I'll be okay with Aunt Alice. She's getting used to my emotional breakdowns. I plan to lose myself in Swan Lake, even if it's just for a few hours."

Alice reached across the table and squeezed Bethany's hand. "We'll be fine. Besides, it's a girls' night. No guys allowed. But thanks for the offer." She dazzled a grateful smile at Steve.

Bethany grabbed her crutches and stood. "Thanks for lunch, Steve. And I'm sorry we took off in such a hurry last night. I'm not normally that skittish. I can understand why the youth love your Boxing Day party. I think I should phone Nat and see if she's still speaking to me. See you later."

"Let me know if there's anything I can do to help," Steve replied with a cheeky grin. "Testy teenagers are my specialty, you know."

Bethany went back to her room and dug the

cell phone out of her purse. She made herself comfortable on the bed and pulled Muffin onto her lap while she dialed Natasha's number.

"Yes?" Natasha answered after one ring.

"Hey, Nat, it's me. Are you speaking to me yet?" Bethany asked tentatively.

"No."

"Oh. Then don't speak, just listen. I'm really sorry about last night. I didn't know I would get so emotional, and I didn't mean to make you uncomfortable. I'm sorry. Still friends?"

"I suppose so," Natasha answered, sounding thoroughly bored by the conversation. "Just don't ask me to hang out with that bunch of losers again. They're so not my type."

Bethany was shocked. *Is that how I sound when I talk about church people?*

"Nat," she began. "Don't be like that, okay? I love my aunt, and these people have been really nice to me."

"Fine," quipped Natasha. "But don't expect me to get all religious just because you are. I have no need for God and neither do you. We have fabulous friends, we're beautiful, and we both have oodles of money. Sorry to be tough on you, Beth, but I think you're going a bit soft."

Bethany breathed into the phone. Finally, she found her voice. "Nat, I have to go. I've got a lot of thinking to do. I'll call you tomorrow. Take care."

"Bye, Beth."

Why does everything have to be so complicated? Bethany thought as she threw her phone to the end of the bed. *I just want to get up and dance to clear my head. I hate my leg. I hate my life.*

She turned on her IPod and stretched out next

to Muffin. Not tired enough for a nap, she spent the early part of the afternoon thinking, analyzing her life, her future, and her dreams. So much had changed for her but one thing still remained—her love of ballet. She pulled open her sketchpad and grabbed a pencil from the dresser. If she couldn't dance with her own legs, she would draw what she felt.

A knock on her bedroom door made her jump.

"Bethany?" Alice called softly.

"Come on in," Bethany said, looking up from her sketchpad.

Alice poked her head around the corner and smiled.

"I'm glad to see you're drawing again. You have a real talent for it, just like your mom. I got the writing gene but I always wanted to draw like her."

Bethany smiled sadly. "It was her way of relaxing. I figured if I can't dance right now, I'd sketch the moves instead."

"Hey, talking about moves," Alice said. "We'd better get moving here. It's nearly four o'clock already. Do you want some help getting dressed?"

Bethany slid the book under her bed and hobbled over to the closet.

"No, thanks. I think I'll be okay. I have this burgundy taffeta dress that's long enough to cover most of my cast. I think I'll pile my hair up with just a few wisps falling down. That takes care of my crazy curls. I'll give you a shout if I need a hand. How about you, Aunt Alice, what will you wear?"

"I have a little, black velvet dress I can dig out. It'll look lovely with the necklace Steve bought me for Christmas. Well, I'll leave you to it."

When Alice left, Bethany turned to Muffin and muttered, "She is head-over-heels about that guy."

An hour later, a very stunning Bethany, and a glamorous Alice, were about to leave when Alice's cell phone rang.

"Hello," she chirped. "Really? No way." Her eyes grew wide and her hand flew to her face. "Bethany, open the front door and take a look outside."

Bethany pulled open the door, and as a frosty wind blew in, she peered out to see a horse-drawn sleigh on wheels, complete with jingle bells and cozy blankets.

"Wow!" was all she could manage to say. "What's going on?"

Alice closed her phone and helped Bethany down the driveway to the waiting horses. "That was Steve. He wanted this to be a special evening for us, so he kept the horses and sleigh for an extra day. We get to travel in style tonight."

Alice squealed in delight and Bethany joined in.

The evening was quite spectacular. The sleigh took them to *Ricardo's* where they enjoyed a delicious Italian meal and some deep conversation. Her aunt listened while Bethany opened up to her about her frustrations with Natasha. Alice spoke about her mission trips to Mexico, and how she would like to take Bethany with her one day. When it was time to head to the theater, the sleigh was waiting for them in the parking lot, and Bethany relaxed as she snuggled into the warm blankets for the short ride.

"Penny for your thoughts," whispered Alice.

Bethany smiled and said, "You know, I think Mom and Dad would be really pleased to know you brought me to see Swan Lake. Thank you." She reached over and kissed her aunt's freezing cheek. "Hey, we're here already. I'd better grab my crutches."

They hurried inside, where the foyer bustled with well-dressed people, grateful to be in from the cold. Bethany looked around and recognized several adults, acquaintances of her parents but she managed to avoid eye contact.

Alice took Bethany's arm, and found their seats. "Thanks for thinking of my leg," Bethany said. She made herself comfortable at the end of a row. "It's nice to be able to stretch it out in the aisle."

Alice passed Bethany a program and smiled. "Let's relax and enjoy this, honey. I'm going to imagine it's you dancing up on that stage. One day, it will be. I'm sure of it."

Bethany shivered at the thrilling thought and carefully pawed through the program, taking note of the ballerinas' names and biographies. In no time, the orchestra had warmed up, and the lights went down.

She took a deep breath when the huge, black curtains opened, and suddenly she was in a different world. Taken in by the swell of the timeless music and the magical beauty of the ballet, Bethany was happy.

It might just only last for a few short hours, she thought, *but I am going to allow myself some joy.*

Watching the prima ballerina, Bethany wondered whether she would ever reach her childhood goal of dancing the lead role in a ballet. Her mother always encouraged her to reach for the stars and dream big but now her confidence wavered. She didn't know if she would ever have the courage to follow her heart again.

She took her eyes from the stage momentarily and looked at her broken leg. Surely she would dance again, wouldn't she? As one of the top dancers in her class, Bethany never considered another path for her future than to be a ballerina. She subtly wiped a solitary tear from her cheek, and with a deep breath, turned her focus back to the stage. Her mother would have wanted her to take in every magical minute of the ballet, and that is exactly what she would do. She secretly imagined her mother sitting right next to her, squeezing her hand at the most exhilarating moments. This was her evening to pretend everything was normal and happy again.

The hours passed in a beautiful blur, and Bethany sighed deeply when the final curtain fell.

"Aunt Alice," she said, and reached for a hug. "That was absolutely stunning. Thank you so much."

Alice's eyes brimmed with tears, as she laughed and hugged Bethany. "You are so welcome, honey," she replied. "I enjoyed it, too. And I imagined you dancing as Odette, which made it even better. Let's go see if our sleigh awaits us."

Bethany shivered as the chilly night air penetrated her wool coat. Sure enough, the sleigh was waiting right outside the theater entrance and drew the attention of many people rushing to their cars.

Bethany pulled the fur blanket up around her shoulders and settled in next to her aunt. She suddenly felt chilled by more than the winter wind. Memories swamped her as she flashed back to the night of the accident. Even though they were at a different theater, memories of that night lay heavy on her heart.

"All set?" Alice asked. "Bethany, are you feeling sick? You're shaking all over."

Bethany felt streams of tears on her face but forced a reassuring smile. "I think I'm all right. Just those memories again. I remember feeling so joyful and content after seeing the Nutcracker with Mom and Dad. It was my birthday, and everything was so perfect. What if we have an accident tonight and something happens to you, Aunt Alice?"

"Bethany," Alice said tenderly. "Nothing is going to happen to us. We'll be home before you know it." She took a breath and continued, "I'm praying for you, honey. God loves you so much. Please don't be afraid."

Alice's words echoed in Bethany's mind when they arrived home. *Will I ever feel safe again? How can I not be afraid after everything has been taken from me? Does God really love me? Really?*

Thoughts of Odette being changed into a swan made Bethany wonder what she was being changed into. And what would become of her.

~ TWELVE ~

The next morning, Bethany puttered around in the kitchen long before Alice was up and about. A chorus of obnoxious birds interrupted her dreams, so she decided to make herself useful by preparing breakfast while Alice slept in. The smell of freshly brewed coffee filled the air, and although Bethany disliked the taste, she loved the rich aroma. She found frozen waffles, which she toasted and doused with maple syrup and canned peaches.

"Not bad, Bethany," Alice said with a smile, standing at the entrance to the kitchen. "I think I'll sleep in more often. This smells scrumptious."

"Thanks," Bethany replied, and hobbled to the table with the plates. "I was up early for a change, so I thought I should earn my keep. Plus, I was starving."

"Well, sit down," Alice insisted. "I'll bring the coffees. Hey, I thought you didn't drink coffee."

Bethany smiled mischievously. "I don't. But it smells so good. I frothed up some hot milk and added a little coffee and a lot of maple syrup. It's my pretend coffee."

The pair dug into their breakfasts hungrily. Immediately, Muffin was at Bethany's chair, sitting on his hind legs, his head to one side.

"Muffin," Bethany laughed. "Could you possibly look any cuter? Here, just one crumb." She held a morsel of waffle in the palm of her hand, which Muffin devoured in a split second.

"You look really good this morning, Bethany," Alice said. She wiped her hands on a napkin before petting Muffin's head. "I'm glad you're doing better than last night. A good sleep always helps. How's the leg?"

"It's about the same, I guess," Bethany began. "But I want to apologize. I didn't mean to spoil
the end of a beautiful evening. I loved the ballet and
the dinner was wonderful. I have to thank Steve for
the amazing transportation. I guess I'm still taking
baby steps, and every now and then, I have to just
let it all out."

"And that's the right thing to do, honey. I
don't want to push you too fast in this healing process but I don't want to hold you back either. I think
it was good for you to immerse yourself in the ballet, and I absolutely understand why you were so upset afterward. There's nothing to be sorry for.
You're doing so well."

When the phone rang, Alice excused herself
and went to the living room to answer. Bethany finished her waffle, and heard her aunt talking in
hushed tones in the other room. When Alice returned
to the kitchen, she looked a little concerned but
covered it with a smile.

"That was Doctor Thomson from the hospital," she said. "He wants to see us this morning at
eleven to discuss your x-ray results. I guess they took
a little longer to process with the holidays and everything."

Bethany felt her stomach drop. "Is there anything wrong with them, Aunt Alice?"

"I honestly don't know, honey. They can't say
anything over the phone but I'm sure everything will
be okay. Doctor Thomson is excellent. Anyway, I'll
get cleaned up in here while you get ready." Alice
hugged Bethany. "Don't worry. We need to see how
that leg of yours is doing, that's all."

"I know," Bethany sighed and left the kitchen. "I just hate hospitals."

An hour later, Bethany sat rigidly in a beige, plastic chair outside Doctor Thomson's office at the hospital. Alice checked in with the nurse at reception and joined Bethany in the next seat. Two small boys played quietly with a wooden train set in the corner. Several adults sat staring into space or reading magazines. There was an air of doom filling the space, and Bethany felt like running away at full speed. That wasn't going to happen anytime soon though, she reminded herself.

Alice flicked through the pages of a gardening magazine, and Bethany tried thinking positive thoughts. Maybe she would be given a date to have her wretched cast removed. A small glimmer of hope ignited within her when she imagined the freedom of not having her leg encased in the ugly cast.

Some nights, the itching around her knee drove her crazy, even with the aid of Aunt Alice's knitting needle. Oh, to be able to bend her knee and practice dance routines again. But then, the antiseptic smell brought back ugly memories of her recent stay. Thoughts of Tim Bennett popped into her head and she briefly wondered if he was still in the hospital.

Was it really only three short weeks ago my life was turned upside-down? So much has happened...

"Bethany St. Clair?" called a young nurse with red hair. She locked eyes with Bethany and smiled. "Doctor Thomson will see you now. Come on in."

Alice helped Bethany up, and they both entered the doctor's office. The room was taupe, plain and smelled of licorice.

"Hello, Bethany. Good to see you, Alice,"

Doctor Thomson said, as he stood up behind his desk. "Won't you both have a seat?"

Bethany eased herself into the comfortable chair and looked at the doctor, trying desperately to gauge whether the news was good or not. She saw him regularly during her hospital stay and always found him friendly. He looked tired today, probably too many nightshifts. She noticed Aunt Alice fidgeting next to her while the doctor shuffled the stack of papers in front of him.

"So, Bethany," he began in his personable, yet efficient voice. "How have you been since I saw you last?"

Bethany detected a trace of sympathy and realized he must suspect how hard Christmas had been for her.

"I got through the holidays," she explained. "It was tough but Aunt Alice has been wonderful." She turned and gave her aunt a grateful smile, then continued, "I'm getting frustrated with my leg though. To be honest, I was hoping it would have started to feel good by now. I hate having to take the painkillers. I guess I'm just frustrated not being able to dance and everything. I can't wait to get rid of this cast."

"Hmm, yes." Doctor Thomson looked at Alice and then down at his papers. "Bethany, I've been looking through your x-ray results, and I'm afraid we still have a little work to do."

Bethany held her breath and let her aunt do the talking for her.

"What do you mean exactly?" Alice asked. She reached over and clasped Bethany's hand. "Surely not more surgery?"

Doctor Thomson stopped shuffling the papers

and looked directly at Bethany. "I know you have been through an awful lot. More than anyone should. You are truly a brave young lady but there is another surgery we need to perform."

Bethany closed her eyes as the room started to spin. Just when she thought things had started to turn around, when life was starting to feel slightly bearable.

"How long will it be until I get back to normal, Doctor Thomson?" Bethany asked. "I just want to dance. I *have* to dance." Tears tumbled down her cheeks and she brushed at them, trying to hold herself together and listen to the doctor.

"It's hard to say, Bethany." The doctor's tone was solemn as he clasped his hands on top of the desk. "I want to be honest with you. I know dancing is a major part of your life, and this must be terribly difficult. But the fact is, even with the surgery, I can't guarantee you'll able to dance like before."

Bethany's mouth went bone-dry and she could hear her pulse in her ears. Aunt Alice and the doctor were talking, but it was muffled, and Bethany couldn't make out the details. She heard "severe break" and "multiple fractures" and "several months." It was more than she could bear. She just wanted to go home. She looked up and saw that Doctor Thomson had asked her a question.

Flustered, Bethany blew her nose and looked at her aunt in desperation. Alice stood and assured the doctor they would get back to him later in the day, once Bethany calmed and could think clearly. The doctor walked around and held the door open for them. Bethany sniffled and hobbled her way to the door, then peered up at him with swollen eyes.

He looked at her kindly, and said, "I'll do everything I can to give you your life back, Bethany. Hang in there."

Bethany's heart was breaking. She couldn't promise him anything.

~ THIRTEEN ~

Bethany moved on her crutches as fast as she possibly could. She had to get out of the hospital, the place where she received nothing but devastating news.

"Bethany, slow down," Alice pleaded, trotting alongside. "I know you're upset but either you're going to slip, or I'm going to fall flat on my face trying to keep up with you in these heels."

"I have to get out of here," Bethany cried while they hurried through the lobby.

The walls seemed to be closing in and she needed to be out of this nightmare. By the time they crossed the parking lot and reached the car, Bethany was soaking wet and utterly exhausted.

Alice dug frantically for the keys in her purse. "I can't believe it's raining. It was lovely earlier on," she muttered.

"I can," replied Bethany. "Everything goes wrong for me. Maybe I'll get lucky and catch pneumonia and die."

Bethany saw the shock on Alice's face. Her aunt opened the car door and helped Bethany get settled before rushing around to let herself in.

Alice slid into her seat, and said softly, "Please don't say that, honey. I know things seem bad right now, but we'll get through it. He's a good doctor, and he knows how important dancing is for you."

"No, he doesn't," Bethany yelled. "He doesn't understand and neither do you. Only Mom knew how important it was for me. And now she's not here to help me."

"I'm sorry," Alice said tearfully. "But I'll try

my best. Let's get you home. Steve should be arriving soon. Maybe you can talk to him. He's a good listener."

Bethany rolled her eyes but then felt guilty. Poor Aunt Alice only wanted to help. She was probably praying for her right now. For some reason, that annoyed Bethany, and she found her deep sorrow and frustration gradually transform to anger. By the time they arrived home, she was feeling a full-blown rage ready to blow. She wasn't sure exactly whom she was angry at but the list was growing. There were the surgeons for having to do another operation, Doctor Thomson for having such bad news, Aunt Alice for being so nice, her parents for not being here, and finally, God for just about everything.

Sure enough, Steve was waiting in his van outside Alice's house. Bethany gathered her crutches when they pulled into the driveway. She threw Steve an angry glare as he stood outside her car door with an umbrella.

"I don't need an umbrella," she shrieked. "I'm already soaking wet."

She followed her aunt into the house without looking back at Steve. Once inside, she shrugged out of her wet jacket and tugged off her one fur boot.

"Honey," Alice said gently and put a hand on Bethany's shoulder. "Come and sit by the fire. I'll make some tea and we can talk this through."

"Fine," Bethany replied through clenched teeth. She collapsed onto the couch with a sigh. "But if either of you tell me everything's going to be okay and that I need to calm down, I'll scream."

Steve closed the front door behind him, hung up his coat, and sat down opposite Bethany. "Thanks, Alice," he said quietly. "Tea would be great."

Alice slipped into the kitchen, and Steve leaned forward, his elbows resting on his knees.

"So I guess things didn't go so well at the hospital, hey? You want to tell me what happened?"

Bethany was all out of tears but she was more than ready to lash out at somebody. Steve was the perfect victim.

"You could say that," she sneered. "My doctor informed me this stupid leg needs more surgery. I'm not going back in that hospital. I hate it there. It brings back the worst memories you could possibly imagine.

"I bet Tim Bennett is doing just fine now, probably home from his hospital stay, getting on with his life. His future hasn't been ruined forever. He still has his mother to look after him and love him. It's just not fair. Where's my mother when I need her? Why can't my leg be better? All I want to do is dance, and Doctor Thomson said I may never be able to dance again."

Bethany's voice reached screeching point as Alice slipped into the living room and sat on the arm of Steve's chair.

"No, Bethany," she began softly. "Doctor Thomson didn't say you'd never dance again. He just warned us that he couldn't guarantee you would dance at the same high level. But you're a fighter. I know you are. Look at what you've overcome already."

"I want my mom and dad." Bethany sobbed into her hands. "Why does God have to take everything away from me? Tim Bennett gets to live while both of my parents died. And now I can't even dance?" She looked up at Steve and asked, "You and

God are pretty tight. You must have some answers. So answer me *why*?"

Steve remained calm while Alice went to comfort Bethany. "I don't pretend to have all the answers," he began. "Only God Himself knows everything. I do know that Tim is a broken young man since the accident. He can't go back to his mother's home because he feels just wretched about the accident, especially with your house being right next door."

"I don't want to see that man. *Ever*," Bethany shouted. "The more I think about him, the angrier I feel. I can never forgive him, I'm sure of that."

Silence filled the living room until Steve looked into Bethany's eyes and said, "You are hurting so much, Bethany. But you are very precious in God's sight, and He loves you more than you can possibly imagine."

"Stop," Bethany cried and stood up. "Just stop. I don't even care anymore. My life is over and I'd better get used to it. You can believe in God all you want but I don't want to hear another word about Him. Not from you or Aunt Alice, or Todd, or Sara. Natasha was right. I don't need God. My world has collapsed and He doesn't care. So neither do I."

Bethany swung around and limped down the hallway to her bedroom, slamming the door with all her might. Muffin was nowhere to be seen and she was totally alone. She had shut out everyone in her life. It felt good. Empowering. She didn't even feel guilty. In the solace of her room, she could think about her miserable life and how it was on a steady downward spiral. She could almost feel herself being sucked farther down by the minute, and she let herself fall.

In an effort to take out her frustration, she grabbed the sketchpad from under her bed, and started ripping the pages to shreds. Pencil drawings of ballerinas and watercolors of ballet shoes, all torn to pieces. It felt good. Nat would understand how she felt. Dancing was her whole life, too. So she pulled the cell phone out of her purse and dialed Natasha's number.

"Yes?" Natasha answered impatiently.

"Nat, it's me. I'm not doing so well," Bethany admitted in a small voice. "I went to the hospital today, and they have to do more surgery. I may never be able to dance like before."

"Beth, that's awful," gasped Natasha. "Will you have to go to another school?"

"Oh," sniffed Bethany. "I hadn't even thought of that. I just don't think I can take it, Nat. I'm tired of it all. You know how dancing is my life, just like it is for you."

"Hey, Beth," Natasha interrupted. "I've got to go. I'm at the mall with the girls. I'll tell them your news. It's just horrible. Speak to you later, okay?"

"Sure," Bethany replied in a whisper and put the phone down on the bed.

"Bethany?" Alice called softly through the closed door. "Do you want some tea? Or maybe something for lunch? I'm worried about you, honey, and I want to help."

"I don't want tea," Bethany snapped. "And I don't want company. I need my space, so please, just leave me alone."

Several seconds of silence followed, then Bethany heard her aunt sniffling and Steve called out, "That's okay, Bethany, we'll give you your space. But we're here for you when you need us."

Bethany didn't give them the courtesy of a response, and soon their footsteps retreated to the kitchen. Nice, even footsteps—not hobbling, limping ones like hers. What if she had a limp for the rest of her life? What if she agreed to this surgery and it didn't work? The thought of not being able to pour everything onto the dance floor was more than Bethany could handle.

Her phone beeped in her hand, indicating a saved voicemail. Curious, she dialed to find out if Natasha had phoned back to be a bit more sympathetic. But it wasn't Nat's voice.

"Hi, Bethany. It's me, Sara. Listen, don't be mad but your aunt called me earlier and told me about your doctor's appointment today. She just wanted me to pray for you. I'd really like to come over and see you, make sure you're all right. Call me, okay?

Why did Sara have to be so nice? And why did so many people have to be praying for her? She didn't want prayers. She wanted her parents and a leg that would give her back the gift of dance.

As a volcano of fury, fear and frustration threatened to erupt within her, she spotted something on her dresser. Something that might be the answer she was looking for. Something to take away the sorrow, the tears, and the ache in her heart.

Right there before her, lay a full bottle of painkillers.

~ FOURTEEN ~

Bethany's hand shook as she reached for the large plastic bottle. She clutched it tightly and closed her eyes. This would be the best way for everyone.

Without Bethany, Aunt Alice would be free to continue her vibrant life. She could marry Steve and start a family of her own. Have cousins Bethany would never meet. Poor Aunt Alice. Her life had been tainted with death, first her own parents, then her sister and brother-in-law, and now her niece. But she was a strong woman with a faith that could move mountains. Bethany felt a prickle of jealousy. Why couldn't she be as strong as her aunt? How could Alice find joy and peace amidst the fiercest of storms?

Bethany's arms felt empty without Muffin nestling in her lap. He had been such a devoted little fluff ball, listening to her many woes and dramatic meltdowns over the past year. A lone teardrop trickled down her face, and Bethany found a measure of comfort knowing that Muffin would always have a home here. He would be safe and well loved his whole life.

Then her thoughts drifted to Natasha. Her dear friend who shared so many sleepless sleepovers, fun vacations, boy dilemmas and ballet dreams. She was self-absorbed for sure but she would even admit to that, with a shake of her long, blonde silky hair. She was a princess but she always allowed Bethany into her castle, and at the end of the day, they were the best of friends. She would undoubtedly miss Bethany for a while but things had been strained between them since the accident. Natasha would bounce back to her normal social butterfly self in no time.

Sara, on the other hand, would be truly sad. Even though they had only known one another a short time, she was a sincere girl with a tender heart. She tried so hard to show Jesus to Bethany but it simply wasn't happening. Bethany appreciated her efforts and kindness, but what had Sara's prayers done for Bethany's leg and dream of dancing again? Glancing at the cell phone on the dresser, Bethany felt a stab of guilt.

Sara's message will be the last thing they find on my phone. What if she thinks it upset me enough to take the pills? I can't let her live with that hanging over her head.

Quickly, Bethany erased the message. Done. If only erasing her life could be that simple.

Todd. There he was in her imagination, his warm eyes lit up by the glow of the bonfire. She admitted she had a major crush on the guy, not that it would ever have gone anywhere. He was so devoted, and living for Jesus, their lifestyles would clash at every turn. But what he shared at the bonfire about his life touched her more than anything.

She realized looking back, how close she came to actually opening up to God. She almost sensed herself softening. But that was before today, before her world came crashing down around her. Again.

How Bethany longed for a hug from her mom and a kiss from her dad. Simple gestures that she never thought twice about before they left her alone. Now she craved their affection, wanted desperately for them to walk into her room and talk her out of this selfish act she was about to perform. But that wouldn't happen because of one icy night on the same road as Tim Bennett.

She could almost feel her blood boil imagining him recovering nicely. When he found out about Bethany ending her own life, he would feel guilty about the whole thing. But quite frankly, he *was* guilty. It might have been an accident but he'd killed Bethany's parents and wrecked her life and her leg in the process. She couldn't help it. Feelings of pure hatred coursed through her veins at the mere thought of that man. He had no right to be alive.

Bethany realized she was sweating, and her pulse seemed to have taken on a crazy rhythm. Enough thinking, it was time to end the pain. The drinking glass on the dresser was empty. She would need water to down as many pills as she could. Lots of water. Bethany put the bottle of painkillers on the bed, limped to the sink in her adjoining bathroom, and filled the glass to the rim.

She turned the faucet off and looked at her reflection in the mirror. What a shame. There before her was an intelligent, pretty girl who several weeks ago had so much to live for. She had dreams of becoming a professional ballerina, of falling in love one day and having a family of her own. But now her dreams were shattered and her hopes ripped out from under her. She reached out and touched her reflection.

"I'm sorry," she said.

Suddenly plagued with regret and feeling horribly nauseous, Bethany slowly and silently made her way out of her bathroom. Through teary, blurred vision, she surveyed the room one last time, and took in the memories she brought with her from her old house.

Her satin ballet shoes hung on the wall next to a framed photograph of her parents. Two tattered teddy bears sat on her French chair, and her mother's jewelry box adorned the dresser. Her skin prickled when she noticed something poking out from beneath her bed.

It was the gold wrapping paper of the unopened birthday gift from her mom. How many times had she nearly plucked up the courage to unwrap it? With nothing to lose, and as a final act of respect, she shakily put down the glass of water, sat on the bed, and picked up the present.

The purple satin bow untied easily, and she tore back the shiny wrapping paper. She gasped at what she held on her lap—a beautiful, handmade scrapbook, just like those in her aunt's living room.

"Oh Mom, you made this with Aunt Alice just for me," she whispered.

As she turned the pages, she discovered each one had been tenderly created with photographs of her life from baby to teenager, nearly all of them in ballet costumes. Aunt Alice always cheered her on and encouraged her in ballet. She even called it a gift from God. And now Bethany was ready to throw away that gift along with everything else, because everything worth living for had been taken from her.

"Sorry to do this to you, Aunt Alice," she whispered. "But you have God to comfort you."

As she turned to the last precious page, her breath caught in her throat. It was a favorite photograph of herself in a white tutu, her arms lovingly wrapped around her mom and Aunt Alice. Underneath, in her aunt's beautiful calligraphy writing were the Bible verses, "There is a time for everything and a season for every activity under heaven...a time to weep and a time to laugh, a time to mourn and a time to dance..."

A time to mourn and a time to dance.

Bethany's heart was breaking. "God," she cried in desperation. "Where are you? I'm frightened. I haven't got the strength to do anything on my own anymore. Help me. I have nothing to live for. I'm so tired, so exhausted. How many tears do I need to shed before it all feels better? When is my "time to weep" going to end so I can have my "time to dance" again?"

As Bethany sobbed and cradled the scrapbook in her arms, a thought troubled her. Had God ever cried? Had He ever felt pain like she was experiencing right now? The sort of pain that is so strong you don't know where it begins or ends?

She strained to see clearly through streaming eyes, and her gaze fell on the tiny Bible Aunt Alice kept on the bedside table. Jesus. Bethany heard enough from her aunt and Steve to know that God's heart had been broken when His Son was crucified. And she guessed God must have felt pretty devastated when His children turned their backs on Him. Like her. Had she caused untold pain for God?

Sliding to the floor, still clutching the scrapbook, Bethany was totally honest with God.

"I hated you and wanted nothing to do with you." She sniffled. "And I am so very, very sorry. I have nothing. I'm empty. I feel like everything has been snatched from me but I'm starting to see that's not true because I have you. Aunt Alice is always telling me that you never leave us and I believe her. I know that Jesus died for me. I guess I've always believed it deep down but now I want to start again, only this time with you in my life. With you in charge of my life. Help me, please?"

As Bethany sat there, an overwhelming sense of peace poured over her, like she was being cradled, too. There was no lightning bolt, no thunderous voice but at that moment, she simply knew that she was a child of God, and that He was going to get her through this. Like Todd, she recognized and accepted the love of the Heavenly Father.

She looked down at the painkillers beside the scrapbook and cried. What had she intended to do? In a moment of desperation and foolishness, she could have ended everything with a crazy overdose. She came so close to making the biggest mistake of her life. She picked up the bottle and quickly threw it to the other side of the room, as if it were on fire.

"I'm so sorry, God," she whispered. "Forgive me."

She opened the book again and stared at the verse. This time, the tears running down her face felt soothing, like they were washing away the pain.

"I know I've got a lot to learn about how Jesus wants me to live and stuff," she prayed. "I know I have to learn to forgive and to love like You do. I'm frustrated and I've never been good at waiting for things, so You'll have to show me how. If you gave me the gift of dancing, like Aunt Alice says, then I'll just have to trust You. "

Bethany knew she should go out and explain to Aunt Alice and Steve what happened. The fact that she nearly made the biggest mistake of her life was nothing to be proud of, but they would be overjoyed to see the peace on her face and the newfound faith that would shape her life from this day on.

But she decided to savor a few more minutes

alone with her Heavenly Father, basking in the light of His love, knowing that now, her grief, her pain, even her beloved dancing was turned over to One who would carry it all. And the ugly heaviness of her shattered young life unraveled from her like a prima ballerina pirouetting across a stage.

~ FIFTEEN ~

The theater lights dimmed and the audience hushed as the music swelled to crescendo. The swish of the velvet curtains sent a chill down Bethany's spine. She stood poised in the wings, ready to make her debut dancing The Nutcracker.

A full year passed since the accident. Much had happened in that time and Bethany knew she matured well beyond her fifteen years. She still thought of her mom and dad every single day, and missed them dreadfully. The "firsts" were tough—the first Valentine's Day without a card from her dad, the first long summer without a family tropical vacation, the first day of a new school year without her mom to cheer her on. But with a growing faith, she was coping well.

She stretched out her right leg and pointed her toe to perfection. The physiotherapy worked wonders. She had taken Doctor Thomson's advice very seriously and taken every precaution to ensure her leg healed in its own time, in spite of her impatience while waiting to dance.

Her school had been extremely accommodating, and Bethany caught up on her studies quickly. She sat in on all the classes even when she was unable to dance, meticulously taking notes to keep up with the others. She realized it was going to take time and a lot more effort to reach the standard she aimed for. But today, she was grateful just to be dancing at all.

Subtly, she waved at Natasha who was in position ready to dance from the opposite wing. Their friendship wasn't quite back to normal. Natasha remained highly put out by Bethany's attendance at

Steve's youth group and church but Bethany wasn't discouraged. She prayed for Natasha every day and had a strong feeling their friendship would be restored, and eventually, Natasha would find hope in God, too.

But today Natasha landed the coveted role of Clara, and was completely engrossed in her ballet. Bethany was proud of her, and even though it had always been Bethany's dream, she counted her blessings, grateful that she was dancing at all.

The two girls still hung out often, and were in the same friend group at school, but Bethany found a more genuine stability with Sara and Todd, and the others from church. In fact, Todd had a special place in her heart, and she dreamed that someday, years from now, they might even have the possibility of a future together.

This evening, Bethany was feeling quite proud of herself. Hers was a relatively small role but she was actually dancing, and that was a miracle in itself. Her heart beat double time when she stole a quick look into the audience. There, in the second row were Aunt Alice and Steve, who finally came to a ballet. Alice looked gorgeous in her long, black evening gown, and once again, she reminded Bethany so much of her mother. Alice had been incredible this year—so patient, nurturing, and fun. To top everything, she now wore a sparkling diamond solitaire on her finger, courtesy of Pastor Steve. She deserved all the happiness in the world.

Things were taking a turn for the better. Bethany took comfort in the fact that Jesus was at the center of her life, orchestrating her every move. Her heart was still mending. There would be seasons of sadness yet to overcome but she found deep-rooted, real joy at last. Some of that freedom was found as a result of reaching out to someone she had unfairly hated with a passion. She had forgiven Tim Bennett.

Bethany picked up the hem of her dress ready to take her first graceful steps on stage, and was overcome with gratitude toward her Heavenly Father. Thoughts of her parents permeated Bethany's mind. She knew they would have been so proud of her this evening. Exhilarated, she took a deep breath and thanked Jesus, for He had turned her sorrow to joy and her tears to dancing.

Dancing that would last for eternity.

~ END ~

About the Author

Laura is married to her high school sweetheart, has three wonderful children, and an adorable English bulldog! Born and raised in England and Wales, she immigrated to Canada in her mid-twenties, and now lives in the beautiful gem of Kelowna, British Columbia, where her authoring dreams have become a reality.

After completing thirteen years of home schooling her children, she is now able to focus on writing, and treasures the privilege of sharing her heart in the form of novels, short stories, and Bible devotions. Laura's strongest desire is to provide wholesome reading with good, solid morals for children, challenging books for teens, and encouragement for adults.

Visit Laura on her website:
http://laurathomasauthor.com

On Facebook:
http://www.facebook.com/pages/Laura-Thomas/183771121724664

And on Pinterest:
http://pinterest.com/lauracthomas/

Made in the USA
Charleston, SC
18 April 2012